Oshun
PUBLISHING

Oshun Publishing Company, Inc.
7715 Crittenden Street
Box 377
Philadelphia, PA 19118

Printed in the United States of America

First Edition: January 2009

10 9 8 7 6 5 4 3 2

ISBN-13: 978-0-9676028-5-1
ISBN-10: 0-9676028-5-8

cover design by Candacek – www.candann.com

visit RAW on the web www.myspace.com/rawnovel

RAW

An Erotic Street Tale

Shay

Oshun Publishing Company, Inc.
Philadelphia

This book is dedicated all those wonderful writers who came before me, and on whose shoulders I stand

Chapter One

"**F**uck it! This shit is taking too damn long," Raheem groaned. "Assume the position, bitch."

19-year-old Chastity rolled her green eyes, as she took Raheem's dick out of her mouth, got off her knees and walked over to the armchair in the corner of the spacious living room. She bent over and pulled up her Armani leather skirt, revealing her silk black Victoria Secret thong then turned her head towards Raheem and licked her lips. "Is this what you want, Daddy? You want to fuck this pussy?"

Raheem grunted, and without a word walked over and pulled the thong to the side with one hand, and used his other to guide himself into Chastity's womanhood. "Yeah, you pretty bitch, that's what I'm talking about," he said as he began thrusting in and out. "Work that shit."

Chastity stifled a yawn. It was a good thing Raheem was already well lubricated from the Lewinsky she had just performed on him, because he didn't even notice that she was dry as all hell. But how the fuck was she expected to be juiced up over a 300-pound gorilla looking motherfucker with a four-inch dick pounding the shit out of her?

"Yeah, Daddy. Take this pussy. You know it's yours. You know it's all yours," she purred as she

5

thought about the shopping spree this fucking was guaranteeing her. That $4,500 leather raincoat she'd been eying at Saks Fifth Avenue was going to be hers. Maybe even a diamond tennis bracelet from Tiffany's like the one Beyonce was rocking at the BET awards.

"Damn right it's mine," Raheem slapped her on the ass. Hard. Pissing her off, and changing her mind from a "maybe" on the tennis bracelet to a "fuck it, that bitch is mine."

She stopped herself from looking at her watch, but managed a furtive glance at the clock on the wall above her head. Shit, almost four o'clock. She wanted to beat the New York City rush hour traffic.

"Ooh, Daddy, you're so damn big you're hurting me," she moaned, throwing her head back and pushing her ass back against his dick. "You're killing me, Daddy. I can't take it."

"You'd better take it, bitch. Take all of your Daddy's big dick," Raheem answered as he always did, forcing Chastity to choke back a laugh.

"Oh, God, you're killing me. You're killing me," Chastity responded. "Oh, but I love it. I love it. Ooh, you're gonna make me cum. I'm gonna cum all over your big fat dick."

"That's right, bitch. Cum for daddy! Cum for daddy!" Raheem yelled, thrusting even harder.

Okay, time to bring it home, Chastity thought. She braced herself on the back of the chair, and stood on her tip-toes to lift her hips as far as she could, then just as Raheem thrust his full four inches inside of her she clenched her pussy muscles tight refusing to let it slide back out, then she twisted her hips in a circle, and screamed: "I'm cumming, daddy. I'm cumming."

6

"Oh, shit, bitch. You making me cum, too! God Damn!!!!!!!!!!!!!!!!!!!!!!"

After a quick shower, Chastity, dressed in a robe, sat in front of the mirror in Raheem's bedroom, brushing her shoulder-length hair and trying to ignore Raheem's plea for her to spend the rest of the day and night with him.

"Why you always got to run, Chas? Damn, you ain't even got a little love for a brutha?"

Yeah, nigga, you might be gangsta in your raps, and you might talk shit when you're fucking, but the real deal is you're just another pussy-whipped motherfucka. "I got mad love for you, Rah, but I've got an appointment at the beauty salon," she lied without batting an eye. "You want me to stay beautiful for you, don't you? And then I promised my sister I'd stop by. It's her husband's birthday and she's giving him a surprise party. Why don't you come?"

"Nah, I ain't got no fucking time for no surprise party for someone I on't even know," Raheem snapped, just as Chastity knew he would. Good thing, too, because Chastity didn't even have a sister. "But damn, girl, don't make me wait another two weeks before I see your pretty ass again."

Chastity walked close to him and rubbed his limp dick through the sweat pants he'd put on after their lovemaking session. "You keep laying it on me like you did today, daddy, and you might never get rid of me." She licked his ear for emphasis.

Ten minutes later Chastity was switching her round ass out of the Fifth Avenue apartment building, "Thanks, Jorge," she said to the doorman who had quickly got off the telephone and rushed to open the door for her. She discretely passed him a fifty-dollar bill,

which he stuffed in his pocket, then strode onto the sidewalk to hail her a cab, enjoying the summer breeze blowing her hair.

"You have a good day, Miss Jones," he said in a heavy Spanish accent as the taxi pulled away.

She reached inside her Fendi bag and pulled out the wad of bills Raheem had handed her as she was leaving. It was always her policy to never count the money her men gave her in front of them -- Legend had taught her that; always act like she was too good to count money, but good enough to deserve a lot – but now that she was alone she was dying to find out what she'd earned by letting Raheem slobber over her for thirty minutes. Nine thousand dollars, not bad, although his stingy ass should have broken her off more. It's not like he couldn't afford it; the last two CD's he produced had turned platinum on the same day they were released, and she knew for a fact that rap artists were paying him upwards of $150,000 for just one of his beats. She was mentally doing her jewelry shopping when her iPhone started ringing. It was Jackie.

"Hey ho. Whatchoo into?"

"Counting my bank. I just left Raheem's," Chastity said while studying her manicure.

"Yeah. What he hit you off wif?"

"What you worried about it for? I ain't breaking you off shit."

"Fuck you, bitch," Jackie said with a laugh. "It's not like I'm hurtin' for any paper. Jerrod just gave me a cool grand for my birthday."

"Yeah? Well, eat your heart out. Raheem just hit me off for nine times that."

"Get the fuck outta here. That's what's up," Jackie said excitedly. "Man, your pussy must be lined with gold or something. You goin' shoppin'?

"I'm on my way to Tiffany's now. Why don't you meet me down there?"

"Can't. I'm here getting my weave done. What you into tonight?"

"This baller I met last week called and invited me to a party at Diddy's. I don't know if I'm going to go, though. I need a night off," Chastity said. "Why? What you got going on?"

"Man, Legend just called me. He's having one of his parties tonight and told me he'd give me two hundred and fifty bucks if I stopped through. You goin'?"

"Damn, that's right. He sent me a text while I was at Raheem's and said for me to give him a call. I guess that's what it was about."

Shit. I sure don't feel like this shit tonight, Chastity thought. But aloud she said, "Yeah, okay. What the fuck. But I'm only staying the hour and then I'm out. I'll give him a call now."

"Naw, naw, Chas. Let me give him a call and say I was talkin' to you and told you about it and you said you'd show and we gonna drive down there together," Jackie said in a rush. "Okay? I need the brownie points."

"Girl, you go ahead and call. I'll swing by and scoop you at midnight, okay? The party won't even be starting for real for real until 'bout then, anyway. But you're going to have to find a ride home if you're going to be working the party, because I'm serious. I'm only staying like an hour. "

"Bet. I'll see you then."

Shay

'Damn, I sure as hell don't feel like going out to Legend's tonight,' Chastity said to herself as she hung up the telephone. Then she fingered her $2,500 Fendi handbag and thought about the money she had redeposited inside. If it wasn't for Legend she probably wouldn't have nine dollars in her bag, but there she was with nine thousand. *Fuck it. I owe him an hour. I owe him a helluva lot more than that.*

It was three years before – shortly after her sixteenth birthday – that her father, a bus driver had been convicted of killing her mother and a crack dealer after he found them in bed together. Chastity knew, and everyone in her Harlem neighborhood knew, that her mother had been fucking around with Big Kev, everyone – that is – except Chastity's father.

"Damn, that's some fucked up shit," her best friend Jackie had said, when trying to comfort an hysterical Chastity after the police had arrested her father. The two teenagers were in Jackie's mother apartment two floors below the apartment where Chastity stayed with her parents, which was now cordoned off with yellow police tape. "Whatchoo gonna do now, Chas? You ain't got no aunts or uncles you can stay with?"

Chastity shook her head. "Nope. Both my parents were only children."

"Yeah, well, you know you can stay here tonight, but my moms ain't even gonna be tryin' to think about takin' you in. Shit, her welfare check and

foodstamps don't barely cover the seven we already got livin' here."

"Yeah, I know," Chastity said, as she started crying again. "I don't know what I'm going to do."

"Well, shit, I know you don't wanna end up in no foster home. They be rapin' people's ass in there," Jackie said.

"Oh, hell, Jackie. What am I going to do?" Chastity started crying harder.

"Look, I know where you might could get a job," Jackie said, rubbing Chastity's back. "There's a new underground spot opened up on 143rd Street, and the word is they's looking for dancers and the younger the better. With your shape and them green eyes I bet you get hired on the spot."

"You gotta dance naked?"

"Yeah, but who cares? You ain't gotta fuck no one, you just gotta dance."

Chastity shook her head again. "Uh uh, I know too many people who starting out just dancing and ended up whores."

Jackie shrugged. "I'm just sayin', is all. Cause I bet you'd get enough bank to get your own apartment and shit."

"Yeah, but I don't know," Chastity said slowly. "I wanna go ahead and finish school and –"

"Damn, girl. Ain't nobody said nuttin' about you havin' to drop out your precious school. Just get some bank so you can take care of yourself while you go. Shit, if you go try out I'll go with you. And then we can get an apartment together like we always talked 'bout. And I promise you I'll make sure you get up every morning and go to school."

11

"Yeah, right. And who's going to make sure you get up?"

Jackie waved her hand dismissively. "Look, Chas. You can trust me on it, okay? School don't mean shit to me, but I know how you be feelin' 'bout it. Shit. You in one of the best high schools in the city, even if it do got you talkin' like a white girl, most of the time."

"There you go with that white girl, shit –"

"Will you fuckin' let me finish? Shit! I'm just sayin', I know it's important to you and since you my girl, I got your back. I promise I'll get your ass up. Now what time we goin' to the spot so we can them dancin' jobs?"

But the girls' plan didn't matter. Not an hour later there was a knock on the door, and a social worker from Child Welfare said she was there to take Chastity away.

She was placed in a foster home run by a kindly middle-aged woman who instructed her to call her Aunt Daisy. Life was okay at first, she had her own room, and made new friends quickly in the Queens neighborhood, but six weeks into her stay Aunt Daisy's boyfriend Jim – a long-distance truck driver – returned to town.

"Now ain't you something," he said when he first set eyes on her, "with all that long pretty hair and them chinky green eyes."

"She is a pretty little thing," Aunt Daisy agreed cheerfully. "Remember when I was her age, Jim? I had a little waist and big hips just like her. She's a lot taller than I was, though."

"Yeah, but she ain't never had them green eyes. And she sure as hell ain't them big tits like you, girl," Jim said in his slow southern drawl when Aunt Daisy went into the kitchen to fix dinner, "all perky and just

12

asking to be sucked. Anyone ever suck them big tits before?"

Chastity spent most of the next few weeks avoiding Jim, and she couldn't swear to it, but it seemed that Aunt Daisy did her best to help in the effort. Whenever Jim came around, Daisy would encourage her to go outside with friends, or make sure they were never alone in the room together. Three weeks after Jim's return home, to Chastity's relief, he announced he was heading back out on the road – hauling a load of chandeliers to Florida. Aunt Daisy made a big production of making him a large going-on-the-road dinner the night before his departure, and went downstairs to kiss him goodbye as he drove off. That night Aunt Daisy went to church Bingo, and Chastity was in her room studying for an American History test when she heard a key turn in the door.

"You forgot something, Aunt Daisy?" Chastity yelled, as she flipped a textbook page.

"It's me," Jim yelled from the living room. "Girl, you seen my wallet? I got all the way to Maryland before I realized I didn't have my damn driver's license."

"No, sorry, I haven't seen it." Chastity sat up in the bed and closed her book. She looked at her open bedroom door, and was just getting ready to get up and shut it when Jim appeared in the doorway.

"You sure you ain't seen it? Where's Daisy?" he demanded.

"At church playing Bingo," Chastity said nonchalantly, trying to ignore the way he was staring at her, as if she didn't have a stitch of clothes on.

"Playing Bingo, huh?" He stood there for a moment stroking his chin. "Well," he said finally, "why

13

don't you come on out here and help me look for it so I can get out of here?"

"I wouldn't know where to look," Chastity said nervously.

"Well, neither do I. Come on and just help me look in the living room. That's the last I remember seeing it," Jim urged. "Come on now, because I'm in a hurry. I've already lost almost a whole day on the road."

Reluctantly Chastity got up and walked to the doorway, but Jim blocked her path. "You know, you never did answer that question."

"What question?"

"You ever let anyone suck them big tits of yours?"

Chastity bit her lip, wondering what to say, if anything. Deciding actions speak louder than words, she gave him a shove in the chest, toppling him backwards, and then tried to close and lock her bedroom door. But Jim was too quick. He pushed his way into the room and grabbed Chastity's arm, twisting it behind her back.

"Why you had to lay your hands on me, huh? I ain't did nothing but ask you a damn question."

"Let go of me!" Chastity shouted.

"I know what your problem is. You just wanna play hard to get." Jim laughed, and then grabbed her by the hair and brought her face up close to his. "Shit, girl. Why you tryin' to act all innocent? With tits like that and them big hips you know you been fucking for awhile. What? You want me to pay for it? I got money. I'll pay."

He tried to kiss her, but Chastity twisted her face away. When he tried again, she bit him on the lip, drawing blood.

"Ow, you little bitch!" he cried, momentarily letting her go. Chastity tried to make it out the door but he grabbed her by the collar of her shirt and dragged her over to the bed.

"I said, let me go!" Chastity screamed, and tried to bite him again. He backhanded her, and she fell onto the bed. When she tried to get up, he punched her in the face. Dazed, she struggled to remain conscious, but she could feel him tearing away her shirt, and then her bra.

"Yeah, they just as pretty as I thought," he said grinning as he roughly fondled her breasts. "Just as pretty as I thought."

"Please, just let me go," she managed to say while trying to push him away.

He laughed. "Girl, you know you want this just as much as me. I seent the way you be looking at me."

"No, I haven't," she protested.

In answer he punched her in the jaw, and when she went limp, he managed to pull down her pants, then unzipped his own and lay on top of her.

"No, get off of me. Please, get off." She started flailing at him, but he ignored her until she tried to bite him again. This time he grabbed by the throat, squeezing until she couldn't breathe.

"You like it rough, huh? Yeah, I can do it rough. You like that, huh?" he said while positioning himself between her legs.

"I can't breathe," she managed to croak.

"If I let you go you promise to stop screaming?"

She quickly nodded yes, and he released his hold on her throat. Then he pulled her panties to the side and tried to insert himself inside of her.

Chastity squirmed, trying to get away from him, and dislodging him in the process. "Girl, stay still so we

can do this," Jim said as he placed one hand over her throat again, though he didn't squeeze this time.

"Jim, please don't do this. I'm a virgin. Please don't do this." Chastity said crying uncontrollably.

"Shit, you ain't no virgin. Now stay still before I sock you again."

Though she continued to squirm and cry, he managed to get his penis inside her opening, and tried to push himself in with one thrust, causing her to scream out in pain.

"Oh shit!" Jim actually pulled away, and sat up halfway. "You really a virgin?"

"Yes, yes! I told you," Chastity said through her tears. "Please just let me go."

Jim seemed stunned into silence, and Chastity managed to push him off of her. But before she could get up, Jim placed one hand on her chest pinning her down. "Chastity, I'm sorry, okay? I ain't know you was no virgin. I mean, shit, how you get so developed if you ain't been fucking, girl?"

"I don't know," Chastity whined. "But, please just let me go. I won't tell anyone."

"Well, shit, you ain't got nothing to tell now, do you?" Jim said soothingly. "I mean, I ain't rape you or nothing, now did I?"

Chastity shook her head, no.

"I ain't no rapist. And I sure as hell ain't no child rapist," Jim continued. "You don't worry, girl, I ain't gonna hurt you."

"Thank you," Chastity said, but when she tried to get up Jim, again, pushed her back down. It was then that she noticed that he had his penis in his hand, stroking it up and down. She began to cry softly.

16

"Come on, don't cry. It's just that, I mean, well, I'm a man. And you done got me so worked up I can't just get up and get in my truck and start trying to drive all night It don't work like that for a man. You know what I mean, right?"

Chastity shook her head no, while still crying.

"Well, that's just how it is," Jim said, while still stroking his dick. "Look, why don't you just let me put it in a little bit. Not all the way, I promise."

"No!" Chastity screamed.

Jim clasped his hand over her mouth. "Girl, what I tell you 'bout all that screaming?" He was silent for a moment, then said, "Okay, if you don't want me to put it in, you gotta do something for me to help me out. Just touch it, okay?" He tried to pull one of her hands toward his erection, but she jerked it back.

"Well, you gonna have to do something, girl. I'm telling you, I can't go like this. And you want me to go, right? Well, then just touch it."

Chastity was crying so hard she could hardly talk, but she finally managed to croak, "If I do you'll leave?"

"Yeah, yeah, I'ma leave. Just touch it for me. Come on," Jim urged.

Still crying, Chastity closed her eyes and allowed Jim to guide her hand to his dick. "Oh, yeah, girl," he said as soon as she made contact. "Now put your hand around it and pull it up and down like you seent me do. Yeah, that's right. Pull it up and down. Oh yeah, that's right. Squeeze it harder. Come on, squeeze it harder. Aw, hell yeah." But after about three minutes of her stroking and him moaning, he stopped her.

"Girl, I'm sorry. But I need more than this," he said, a dogged look in his eyes.

Shay

"But you promised!" Chastity said quickly.

"I know, I know, but this just ain't doing it for me. Let me just put it in a little bit. I ain't gonna hurt you. I'm just stick it in a little bit."

"No," Chastity shook her head violently, and started sobbing again. "Please no."

"Come on, girl. I'll even pay you. I'll give you twenty bucks if you just let lay me on top of you for a minute in put right at the crack. Just right at the crack. I won't push it in at all. I promise."

"No, please no."

But Jim was already pushing her back down into a laying position, ignoring her struggling and crying.

"Wait, wait," she said as he was positioning himself between her legs again. "What if I let you put it my mouth? Please. How about do that?" Even she couldn't believe she was saying it. She knew girls in school who talked about sucking their boyfriends' dicks, and she thought they were just plain nasty, but even doing that was better than having him rape her, she decided.

"You wanna suck my dick?" Jim asked, surprise evident in his voice. "You really are a hot mama, ain't you, girl. Yeah, come on, suck me off." He sat up, then took her head and pushed it toward his penis. She closed her eyes again, timidly stuck her tongue out, and gave his penis a quick lick, and almost gagged at the taste of his pre-cum.

"Come on, girl. Do it right," Jim said urgently. "You don't want me to stick it in you them come on and suck me off."

She tried again. This time opening her mouth and wrapping her lips around his penis, and moved her

18

head up and down, but doing her best not to let his penis touch her tongue.

"Come on, girl. You gotta suck it!" Jim pushed her head all the way down on him, forcing her to choke and pull away crying.

"Shit, this ain't gonna work!" He threw her down, and placed one hand on her throat then literally jumped on top of her, knocking the wind out of her, then he pulled her panties to the side and started forcing himself inside of her.

Chastity tried to scream, but no sound came out. The pain was so intense, sharp and blunt pain at the same time. It felt like someone was pushing a dull knife inside of her, tearing her flesh apart. She twisted and turned, trying to dislodge him and stop the assault on her innocence, but he was too strong and too determined. He just kept on pushing. She prayed that she would black out, but her prayers went unanswered as he continued pushing and pushing himself inside of her, grunting and moaning the whole time. Just when she thought she was on the brink of death, he lay still on top of her, panting. Thinking it was finally over, she tried to push him off of her, but he grabbed her hands.

"Look, I'm sorry I hurt you, girl, but I had to get it all the way in so it would stop hurting," he said in a hoarse voice. "Damn you was tight. But now that I got it all the way in it ain't gonna hurt no more, okay? I'm start stroking it in and out, but it ain't gonna hurt. It's gonna feel good, I promise."

"No," Chastity moaned. "I want you to stop."

"I'ma stop real soon," Jim said as he slowly began to move in and out of her.

"Please, you're hurting me." The sharp pain was now replaced by a dull painful throbbing, and was

almost as unbearable. She continued squirming and trying to push him off of her.

"Stop lying. It don't hurt no more," Jim said as he continued his thrusting. "Yeah, keep moving like that. Just like that. Aw shit, now. Oh Jesus Christ. Oh Jesus. Oh yeah, that's it. That's it girl. THAT'S IT!!!"

It was finally over. He lay on top of her for only another minute or so before getting up and fixing his pants. "Girl, I'm sorry I hurt you. But since you was a virgin someone had to do it, and it was gonna hurt anyway so no harm done, right?"

Chastity sat up in the bed, and cradled her face in her hands as she cried.

"Come on, now, girl. Stop all that crying. I said I'm sorry. Look, you want me to get you a glass of water or something? Let me get you a glass of water."

As soon as Jim left the room, Chastity tried to get up to lock him out the room, but when she got up she fell to the floor, her legs too rubbery for her to walk. That's when she noticed the blood dripping down her legs, and pooled on the bed sheets. Her blood. Her virgin blood.

"Look what I found in the kitchen," Jim said returning to the bedroom with a smile and waving his wallet as he tried to hand her the glass of water. "Come on, now, girl. Stop all that crying," he said as he sat on the side of the bed. "I said I'm sorry, right? What's done is done, ain't no use in your still crying about it. And I said I was gonna pay you, right? Well, I ain't never lie." He pulled two twenties and a ten out of the wallet and tried to give it to her, but she turned away. "Well, look, I'ma leave it right here on your dresser. You change your mind it'll be right there for you."

He put his wallet in his pants pocket and was almost out of the bedroom when he stopped again. "Look, you don't need to tell Daisy about all this. This is just between me and you, okay? And I promise when I get back from Florida I'll make it up to you. You'll see, girl. I can be a good friend to you. I'ma take good care of you."

Chastity wiped her eyes, and glared at him. "You can just go to hell," she said with a snarl.

Before he could respond, they both heard the lock turning in the front door.

"Aunt Daisy!" Chastity yelled. She jumped up, and tried to push past Jim, but he pulled her back and strode into the living room in front of her.

"Hey, Daisy," he said as if nothing happened. "Guess what? I had to come all the way back because I left my wallet here. I can't be driving around with no license, you know. Too many state troopers just looking for an excuse to lock a black man up, you know."

"Jim –" Daisy started to say, then stopped as Chastity appeared in the room, wearing nothing but a torn pair of panties.

"Aunt Daisy he raped me!" Chastity screamed, while pointing at Jim. "He raped me!"

"Oh my God, what –"

"Now just calm down, Daisy," Jim said rushing toward the woman. "There's two sides to every story."

"Jim, what –"

"I ain't wanna tell you this, Daisy, but that girl been propositioning me for the longest."

"Aunt Daisy, that's a lie!"

"It ain't no lie, and she knows it," Jim continued calmly. "Then when I came back here to get my wallet and you wasn't here she said she would do me for fifty

bucks. And Daisy, I'm sorry, but I'm a man. And when she started rubbing on me and everything I got weak."

"Aunt Daisy, oh my God, you know he's lying."

Daisy looked at Jim, and then to Chastity, then back to Jim. "I can't believe you would do something like this to me, Jim."

Even through her anger and desperation the words struck Chastity as ludicrous. What was she talking about? He hadn't done anything to Aunt Daisy; it was her he had violated. Her he had raped. Her he had beaten.

"Daisy, you've got to believe me. I'm sorry. But like I said, I'm a man. And when she started coming on to me like that –"

"Aunt Daisy, I didn't come on to him. He came into my room and he raped me." Chastity started crying.

Daisy rushed over to her and took her in her arms. "You poor, baby."

"Daisy, I can't believe you're gonna take her word over mines," Jim said in a frantic voice. "I swear 'fore God I ain't rape that girl. I swear on my mother's grave!"

"Jim, how do you expect me to believe that –"

"Look, come here." Jim pulled Daisy away from Chastity and into the girl's bedroom. He pointed to the fifty dollars he'd left on the dresser. "Where'd she get that money from if she ain't make me pay for it? You in the habit of giving her fifty bucks for allowance or something?"

Daisy's eyes opened wide as she picked up the money and stared at it. She then turned to Chastity, who started crying.

"Aunt Daisy, you've got to believe me," she said between sobs.

22

"Where'd you get this money from?" Daisy asked in a quiet voice.

"Aunt Daisy --"

"I asked you a question, Chastity. Where'd this money come from?"

"He put it there. But I didn't ask him for it. And I told him I didn't want it."

Daisy walked over and slapped Chastity so hard the teenager went reeling into a wall. "You think I'm stupid? You expect me to believe that Jim raped you and then paid you? Do you think I was born yesterday?"

"But, Aunt Daisy, look," Chastity said pointing to the blood on the bed. "I'm telling you he raped me. And I was a virgin."

"Daisy," Jim said quickly. "After we finished and I saw the blood she started laughing and said I had sex with her during her women's time of the month. And you know I wouldn't have done it if I'd known it was her time. You know how I feel about that. Made me feel downright stupid. Dirty, too."

Daisy nodded, then looked at Chastity again, "I opened up my home to you and I treated you like you was my own and this is how you repay me? By seducing my boyfriend? I was good to you, Chastity. I never treated you like a slave or abused you like they do at most foster homes. But you're nothing but a harlot." Her eyes narrowed. "But I shouldn't have expected anything less. Your father is a murderer and your mother was a whore." With that she stormed out the room and into her own bedroom, slamming the door behind her.

"See," Jim muttered after Daisy had gone. "I told you to keep your mouth shut. Now you done ruined everything and got Daisy all upset."

Chastity was silent, dismally reflecting on everything that had just happened in the past hour. Suddenly she looked up at Jim. "How much money do you have?"

"Huh?"

"I said how much money do you have?"

Jim looked at her suspiciously. "I got money. Why?"

"You still want to be my special friend when you get back?"

Jim's eyes narrowed. "What are you trying to do, girl? Tryin' to get me in trouble again?"

Chastity slowly shook her head, a half smile, half snarl appearing on her lips. "No, I'm trying to make the best of a bad situation. You give me three hundred dollars more to keep me going while you're away, and you and I keep being friends when you get back."

"Girl, you serious?"

"Yeah, I promise."

Jim opened his wallet, and pulled out some money. "I only got two hundred more on me. I'll give you the rest when I get back. But don't you goin' tryin' to upset Daisy no more. Ain't no use in getting her any more riled up. Won't do nobody no good."

Chastity waited until 3 a.m., when Jim had left and she could hear Daisy snoring in her bedroom, then slipped out of the apartment, taking her few belongings with her. After a forty-five minute subway ride, Chastity arrived in Harlem.

Chapter Two

"**D**amn, it's 'bout time you got here," Jackie grumbled as she climbed in the passenger seat of Chastity's silver 2008 Mercedes CLK63. "Shit, Chas, you coulda at least called and let me know you was running late. Or at least answered your damn phone when I called."

"Chill, Jackie. It's only 1 a.m. the real party's just getting started," Chastity said nonchalantly.

"Legend's gonna have our ass," Jackie said, snapping her seat belt in place.

"I bet he ain't even call to check on us."

"Naw, he ain't call, but –"

"See what I mean?" Chastity said triumphantly. "He knows he can count on me. Besides, he likes it when we make an entrance at his parties."

"He like it when YOU make an entrance," Jackie said gloomily. "If it was just me he'd be blowing up my cell wondering where the fuck I was at."

Chastity shrugged. "Whatever."

"So what the fuck took you so long?"

"I had to change my clothes."

"Huh?" Jackie turned in her seat and took a good look at Chastity for the first time since getting in the car. "Damn, girl. I thought you said you was gonna wear your Halston pants suit. What the fuck you doing wearing that shit?"

25

Shay

"This shit is a Vera Wang evening gown," Chastity said huffily, smoothing her hand over the red silk and taffeta halter dress, "and it set me back $3,500 the last time I was in L.A., so watch your mouth."

"Why the fuck you wearing a fucking gown to one of Legend's freak parties?"

Chastity shrugged. "Just felt like it. Besides, I wanted to wear something that goes with this," she held up her hand so Jackie could get a good look at the gold charm bracelet on her wrist. "Got it today at Tiffany's."

"God damn, girl! That's what I'm talkin' 'bout." Jackie grabbed Chastity's hand for a closer look. "Diamonds, rubies, and . . . are these emeralds?"

"Damn real."

"How much this set you back?"

"Ten thousand."

"Ten thou . . . get the fuck outta here," Jackie said quickly dropping Chastity's hand. 'It's that, but it ain't all that. I mean, I can see four or five thousand, but I wouldn't be shelling no damn ten thousand for it."

"No?" The car was stopped at a red light, and Chastity quickly unclasped the bracelet and handed it to Jackie. "Put it on for a minute."

Jackie took the bracelet and as soon as she did she gasped. "This shit must weigh five pounds! God damn!"

"Yep. Now open up the diamond heart charm."

"Who's this? Your pop?"

Chastity nodded. "Open up the emerald star charm."

"Legend." Jackie laughed. "It figures. I don't know what you and that nigga got goin' on, but I know y'all got something. Come on, be honest. You fuckin' him, right?"

26

"Naw, Legend and I are just friends. But that's my man. He's always looked out for me, you know that."

"Yeah, I know," Jackie said as she opened up the ruby moon charm. "You ain't put no picture in any of these other charms?"

"Nope. Haven't figured out who to put in the other ones." She pulled over, and pulled out her iPhone. "Legend? Hey darling, it's me. I'll be pulling up in exactly ten minutes. See you then."

"Why you do that?"

"You'll see," Chastity said with a smile.

In precisely ten minutes Chastity's Mercedes pulled up in front of a brownstone on 137th Street in Harlem. Outside stood a group of about seven men, ranging in age from their early twenties to mid-sixties. Their clothes also varied, from jeans and sneakers to Italian suits, but all looked like pure money. There were no parking spots on the street, so Chastity double-parked.

Jackie had already taken off her seat belt and was reaching for the door to get out, when Chastity whispered. "No, just wait a minute."

"Huh?" Jackie had barely gotten the word out when a tall man wearing a blue custom-made suit and a fedora hat walked over and opened the passenger door.

"Ah, Jackie," the man said, holding his hand out to her. "So good to see you this evening."

"Um, thanks,. Legend," Jackie said quickly as he helped her out the car. "Good to be here."

"Gentlemen, may I introduce Miss Jackie Faison," Legend said grandly, waving his hand in the direction of the men who stood gawking at Jackie. Chastity noted with satisfaction that Jackie had outdone

Shay

herself. Her gold metallic dress was tight and short and hugged her curves, but not enough to make her look hoochie, just enough to show off her voluptuous figure. And the six hours she sat in the hairdresser's chair had paid off. Her long flowing weave hung down her back, with not a stray strand out of place.

Chastity waited patiently as Legend made introductions, then smiled as she saw him approaching her side of the car.

"Chastity, my love!" he said as he opened her door and helped her out. "What a pleasant surprise. To what do I owe this honor?"

"Well, when I heard you were giving a party I couldn't resist stopping by," Chastity said graciously as Legend kissed her hand, smiling at the discrete lick of the tongue he gave as he did so. "I hope you don't mind me crashing."

"Mind? Not at all. I'm in awe. And might I say you look beautiful?" Legend held her arm in the air and gave her a little twirl, allowing the hem of her evening gown to flow in the breeze the turn made. It had the desired effect. All of the men who had gathered around Jackie were now silent, and staring at her as if she'd just stepped off a fashion runway. Chastity knew she was looking good, but the stares were the validation she lived for. Her dress was stunning, and her long hair was pulled back into a loose half-bun with a mane flowing down her back, and long tendrils hanging down the side of her cheeks; and the look on Legend's face confirmed that she had made him proud. She was in her glory.

Although she was tall, almost 5'10, she had to stretch her neck to kiss Legend on his cheek, and while doing so she inhaled his magnificent fragrance. It was strange, but no matter what cologne he wore, the scent

28

was always overpowered by the smell of money; as if he printed it for a living. As she leaned into him she couldn't help but smile at the hardness of body, not an ounce of fat evident on his athletic body. His hair was jet-black and naturally straight, and although he normally wore it down on his shoulders, it was now pulled back into a small ponytail, giving him a European look. That's what he looked like, a European movie star, and that's how he carried himself, she noted with satisfaction as she lightly placed her hand on the arm he offered as he led her to the sidewalk. No wonder he was the toast of Harlem. Even celebrities vied for invitations to his parties; and they were willing to pay whatever the cost to be invited to the clandestine entertainment he held in the basement of his brownstone while the not so fortunate guests drank and danced upstairs on the first floor.

"Tommy, would you park Ms. Jones' car?" Legend said to a uniformed valet standing off to the side of the crowd of men.

"Of course, sir."

"And now, gentlemen," Legend grandly said to the group of men, who seemed to be waiting impatiently, "I'm honored to present a good friend of mine, Ms. Chastity Jones."

"How do you do?" Chastity said to each man to whom she was introduced, flashing them an expansive smile, but remaining somewhat aloof, as Legend had taught her to do in these situations. "It's a pleasure to meet you." There was a Hollywood movie producer, an independent movie director, two R&B singers, an up and coming hip-hop artist, and a well-known novelist; all of whom paid lavish compliments.

Shay

"Chastity, it was our good fortune that we just happened to have come outside for a smoke when you and Jackie pulled up," Legend said after the introductions were done. "But I think we're all done, wouldn't you say, gentlemen? How about we rejoin the other guests?"

"Damn, Chas," Jackie whispered as they walked into the brownstone. "I ain't never comin' to another one of Legend's parties less I get a ride with you. A ho can get used to this shit."

Legend had bought two brownstones ten years before, when they were still going for no more than $100,000 each, but when gentrification took place the real estate prices had skyrocketed, and now they were worth more than a million each. One brownstone he kept as his residence, the other he turned into his party house, after making all sorts of expensive renovations which made it worth at least an additional two hundred grand. He had knocked out all the walls on the first floor of the brownstone, and it was expansive as any loft in Greenwich Village. It could easily hold more than 200 people, but because Legends parties were so exclusive there were never more than about a hundred people inside. There were at least that many at this evening's parties, all dancing to the live entertainment – a gorgeous underground hip-hop artist, Takia Miguel, who had recently scored gold on her debut CD.

There was a bar set up in the corner of the large room, and the champagne was flowing as people ordered magnums of Dom Pérignon, Cristal, and Moet for their tables, which were scattered around the sides of the room. Legend bought his liquor by the case on the black market, so he was easily making thousands of dollars

tonight, but still the real money, Chastity knew, would be made downstairs.

"Legend," she said taking him to the side. "What gives? I've never known you to give a party on such short notice."

"Chas, I need a favor. I'm short a girl. Can you work for me tonight?"

She hesitated, prompting him to take her by the arm and say urgently. "Please? You know I wouldn't even ask if I really didn't need you."

"Sure," she said hurriedly, embarrassed that he had noticed her hesitation.

He exhaled. "Thanks, Chas. And I'm sorry for the short notice, but I didn't even know I was giving a party until this morning."

Chastity raised one of her perfectly arched eyebrows. "What do you mean? What happened to make you decide to –"

"You'll see," he said with a secretive grin. "It's a surprise."

Must be a doozy, Chastity thought as she looked around the room, wondering which guests would get the tap on the shoulder – their personal invite downstairs.

She found out an hour later. Legend came over and whispered in her ear, "The entertainment's going to be starting soon." She nodded and headed downstairs to the basement, catching Jackie by the arm and signaling her to follow.

The basement was dimly lit, and like upstairs, there were tables scattered around the room, each containing six chairs. But while there were 20 tables upstairs, there were only ten tables in the basement. Also unlike the first floor, there was a magnum bottle of champagne sitting in a bucket of ice on each table.

31

Shay

Although there were no signs on the table, Chastity knew the deal. Each table had a cover charge. A hefty cover charge. Four of the tables had a cover charge of five hundred dollars per person. Three of the tables were $750 per person, and three cost $1,000. The cost of seating had nothing to do with the location of the table, but the hostess – or table diva – who headed each table. The beautiful table divas hosted five hundred dollar tables; stunningly beautiful girls headed the $750 tables, and the girls who were so unbelievable that you never thought you had a chance to actually meet her in person headed the thousand dollar tables. Chastity, of course, always hosted a thousand dollar table. As hefty as the cover charge was, Legend never had a problem filling the spots, in fact there were always people begging to pay extra to gain entry into the basement. And even after paying the table divas, the floaters like Jackie, and the night's entertainment, Legend cleared about $20,000 on his exclusive basement party – and that didn't take into consideration the money he made on the party going on upstairs.

Seven of the tables already had girls sitting down at them, all with their legs crossed and all looking as good – or almost as good – as Chastity. In fact, Chastity recognized two of them as finalists from the show, *America's Next Top Model*. Three of the girls she knew personally, and she greeted them as she made her way to one of the tables.

"Look at these skanks," Jackie grumbled. "They all think they're so fucking cute with their fake boobs and their colored contact lenses."

"Whatever," Chastity said, not really listening to her friend. "But listen, sit with me for a minute, I just

want to school you real quick on what you're supposed to do."

"School me? Bitch, please." Jackie laughed. "I'm the one who turned you on to Legend's parties, remember?"

"Yeah, but your role's about to change, so now you've got to take lessons from me," Chastity answered.

"What do you mean?"

"You're moving from floater to table diva."

"Get the fuck outta here!" Jackie said excitedly. "Legend's okay with that?"

Chastity nodded. "I talked to him about it upstairs. He's going to let you host one of the five hundred dollar tables."

"Yeah, man, that's what's up," Jackie said, rubbing her hands together. "This is just the break I been wanting for."

"Uh huh, but there's some things you've got to know."

"Like what?"

"Like you have to act like a lady."

"Shit," Jackie waved her hand. "I can do that."

"You can, huh? Well, the first thing is you can't be cursing every other word, or calling the other girls bitches, ho's, or skanks."

"Yeah, yeah, I can figure that much out."

"Okay, good. What separates the table divas from the floaters is the divas don't openly flirt with the men on the table, but they pay special attention to all of them, and make each of them feel special. Laugh at their jokes, smile at them, when you talk to one of them just casually put your hand on theirs, compliment them all, but don't give them all the same compliment. Tell one he smells good. Tell another one you love his suit.

33

Compliment another one on his jewelry. But whatever you do, don't ask them where they bought anything or how much it cost, okay? You want them to feel as if you're impressed with what they're sporting, but also that you're used to being around men who are rocking it like that. Got it?"

Jackie nodded. "Got it." She leaned forward on the table, cradling her face in her hands as she took in the instructions.

"Good. And make sure all of the men at your table are having a good time. If you see the champagne bottle is less than a quarter full, order another one."

"Got it," Jackie said again.

"Now this is important, although you're the star at the table, you can't be selfish. If you see one of them eying one of the floaters, call the floater over and make an introduction."

"Is that how it works?" Jackie said incredulously? "I always thought the table divas just called over the floaters who were their friends. I mean, I always got called over to your table more than any of the others."

"Well, you can give hints." Chastity smiled broadly. "For instance, I might say, 'Jackie is looking really nice tonight. But then that girl always looks nice, don't you think?' or something to that effect."

"You my girl," Jackie said offering her fist for a pound.

"And you know you're mine," Chastity said. "But the thing is, if you notice one of your guests craning their neck looking at another one of the table divas, offer to take them over and make introductions. But don't worry, even if your guest sits at someone else's table, you still get credit for whatever they spend."

34

"Yeah, well, I'm gonna be so fuckin' on ain't none of my guests gonna wanna go nowhere else."

"Yeah, okay, but if they do, follow the rules, Jackie." Chastity's eyes narrowed. "I mean it. If Legend gets any complaints about you after the party is over you're not going to be invited to be a table diva again. And remember, I recommended you, so it's going to be a reflection on me."

"Yeah, yeah, don't worry. I got your back," Jackie said, waving her hand dismissively. "But tell me about the money deal. How do I make my money?"

"Well, forget what Legend promised about two-fifty. You –"

"What? I don't get my two-fifty?"

"Will you shut up and let me finish? Damn, girl!" Chastity laughed. "Since you're at a five hundred dollar table, you'll automatically make five hundred dollars –"

"Yeah, girl, that's what's up!" Jackie said, wiggling her shoulders in excitement.

"And you get five percent of the amount of money they spend on coke and ecstasy."

"Yeah, that'll work! I'm gonna have it snowin' like a blizzard at my table!"

"But you gotta be cool about how you do it," Chastity warned. "You can't suggest to anyone that they buy coke or pills, but what you do is give hints. Like, for instance, nurse your champagne over a long period of time, and when someone asks why you're not really drinking, say something like, 'Well, it's not my high of choice.'"

"It's not my high of choice," Jackie repeated.

"Right. Since they're not allowed to bring their own stashes, if they want to impress you – and if you've

been doing your job right all night, they will – they'll hurry up and buy some shit from one of Legend's people."

"Sweet!"

"And let me give you one of my own personal tips," Chastity looked around to see if any of the other girls were close to hear. "Some of the guys dump their coke in hundred dollar bills, and when they're finished they offer you the bill –"

"Aw, yeah!"

"Well, if they do, smile and say, 'Well, how about you give it to me in a more personal way,' then lean forward so they get a good look at your cleavage, and tap the space right between your breasts. Remember, Legend has a non-grope rule that the men have to follow, so this would be the only opportunity for them to cop a feel. Once you do that for one guy, I guarantee you every nigga at the table will be buying coke. You get your five percent cut off of what they buy, and you get to keep all the bills."

"You watch. I'ma clean up tonight," Jackie said confidently.

"Okay, your table is over there," Chastity said, pointing three tables down.

"I'ma tear it up!" Jackie said as she stood up.

"Oh, one more thing. And this is REALLY important. You cannot give out your telephone number. If someone asks for it, tell them it's against house rules for you to give it out, but that you're sure Legend will give it to them later."

"Why's that?"

"Because Legend will charge them for the number, and he'll give you 50 percent of whatever he makes off it."

"How much does he charge? And how I know he ain't gonna cheat me?"

Chastity rolled her eyes. "Puleeze, like Legend is gotta cheat you to make money. And he charges whatever he thinks the nigga will pay. He's good at sizing up these niggas and coming up with a figure. Don't worry. And if there's anyone who you don't want him to give the number, just let him know."

"Got it."

"Hurry up and get situated at your table," Chastity said urgently. "Legend's coming down now."

Chastity smiled as Legend walked over to her table, with five of the men she'd met outside. She must have really made a good impression since, she found out, they'd all specifically asked to sit with her. .

After everyone was seated, and the usual chit-chat had subsided, Legend walked to the center of the floor, and a spotlight lit up the area in which he stood.

"I'd like to thank all of you for consenting to be my special guests for the evening, and let me assure you that I will do everything to make sure that all of you have a good time. Some of you are here for the first time; some of you have been to my special parties before. But I assure you all, you're in for a extraordinary treat tonight. Take my word for it; this will be a night you won't soon forget."

Legend waited until the applause died down before continuing. "As usual, I ask that all of you abide the house rules, which you all are aware of. And I remind you, no pictures or filming is allowed. However, if you do want a memento of tonight's entertainment, please see me after the show is over, and I'll be glad to arrange for you to obtain a personal video."

"For a nominal charge, of course!" the hip-hop artist at Chastity's table shouted. Well, he just permanently scratched his name off the exclusive party list, Chastity thought.

"But I've talked enough," Legend said, rubbing his hands together. "How about we start the show?"

With that, Legend walked off the floor, and Juelz Santana's latest hit started blaring from the speakers situated throughout the room. And in a few seconds, a tall white woman with stringy blonde hair and a bust that looked to be at least 38DD's danced her way to the center of the spot light. She was wearing a long tight black dress with matching gloves that reached her elbows, and stiletto heels, but the dress and gloves were off within five minutes as she started her slow strip tease; revealing a corset with garters and fishnet stockings. The crowd cheered as the corset came off, and she turned her back and flexed and unflexed her ample ass for their benefit. It took another two minutes for her to finally become stark naked, and the crowd started hooting, clapping, and throwing money onto the floor as she took one of her breasts into her mouth while rubbing her pussy. As the one song went off and another came on, a short woman with flaming red hair edged closer and closer to the spotlight as if she were mesmerized by the first woman. After a few more minutes of the 38DD playing with herself, the red head let out a loud moan, and ran over to the woman, grabbed her kissed her full on the lips. 38DD seemed shocked, and pulled away, but as the red head started doing a strip tease, 38DD woman walked over to her and started licking her on the neck. It all seemed spontaneous, but Chastity knew it was all part of the staged act.

Soon the women were on the floor, and the red head woman was in between 38DD's legs tonguing and eating her out.

"I want more! I need more!" 38DD shouted, in a Russian accent, over the music.

"More?" the red head asked, as if surprised.

"Yes, I need something bigger than your tongue inside this hot hungry pussy!"

"Okay." The red head stood up, sashayed to one of the tables and picked up an empty magnum champagne bottle. "How about this? You think you can take this?"

"Oh, no. No way."

"Ah, so this is too much for you, then?" the redhead asked.

"No, But that's Moet. I only like Dom Pérignon." 38DD said, prompting laughter from the crowd.

The red head picked up a bottle of Dom Pérignon. "You sure you can take it?"

Oh yeah, I can take it," 38DD said. "My pussy is begging for it."

The red head got on her knees and started slowly inserting the bottle into 38DD's pussy.

"Oh, that feels so good," 38DD shouted after half the champagne bottle was inside her. "But I want more!"

"Are you sure?" red head asked.

"Give me more. My pussy's hungry tonight."

"Okay, how about this!" The red head kept pushing until about three-quarters of the magnum bottle was inside, then started slowly pushing the bottle in and out of 38DD. The crowd was going crazy, throwing money and shouting "Give her more! Give her more!"

Shay

"I don't know," the red head said, turning to the crowd. "You really think I should?"

"Yeah, give her more!" the audience responded in what seemed like one voice.

38DD moaned, in what seemed like pleasure, as the red head complied with the crowd's request. It took a few minutes of slow insertion, but soon the whole bottle disappeared inside 38DD. The audience jumped to its feet clapping.

When the cheering finally died down, 38DD started shouting. "Give me more. I want more!"

The red head pulled the champagne bottle from 38DD's pussy, then jumped to her feet. "Well, I don't have anymore," she said, crossing her arms and frowning down at the other woman.

"Well, I do!" A man wearing a long black cape strode over to the women. "She wants more, I give her more!" And with that he threw off his cape revealing a naked body that sported muscles like LL Cool J, and a dick that hung down to his knees.

The audience went crazy again. "Oh my God," someone shouted. He's gotta be about 14 inches.

"Sixteen!" the man shouted back proudly.

Now this is a show, Chastity thought as she felt herself getting moist as 38DD started giving the man a blow job while the red head played with his balls. In no time at all the man was fully erect, and the red head pulled a weight bench onto the stage. 38DD lay down on the bench, with her pussy at the edge as if she were on a GYN table, and the man positioned himself in front of her spread eagled legs. Almost all of the audience left their tables to crowd around the stage to get a better view as the red head guided the man's dick to the 38DD's

crack, and he started to slowly push his way in her pussy.

"Is this enough?" he shouted when he was halfway in, which meant he'd already given her about eight inches.

38DD didn't have to answer, the crowd responded for her. "Give her more!"

38DD moaned and twisted her head from side to side as the man started pushing himself in further. He was about three-quarters of the way in, when he stopped, taking a deep breath as if to calm himself, before saying: "You want more?"

"Give her more!" the crowd responded.

"Give me more!" 38DD agreed. "My pussy's hungry for more!"

The man started again, slowly inserting himself in, but he wasn't fully in another inch when his eyes closed, and his face scrunched up, and all of a sudden he thrust his full length inside her pussy, and he started slamming against her fast and hard.

38DD's eyes and mouth flew open, and she looked like she might be experiencing some discomfort, but she managed to keep up with his rhythm. It was over in just a few seconds as the man let out a groan and slammed into her full force, then collapsed on her stomach.

The crowd went wild, clapping and stamping their feet, and shouting. "Yeah, I bet she don't want no more after that."

The red head, who had been standing off to the side playing with herself, went to the 38DD's side and bent down and appeared to ask the dazed but smiling 38DD something. Suddenly the red head stood up and shouted, "She says she wants more!"

41

A gasp went out through the crowd. "Now that's a freak," someone shouted.

Another one yelled. "This shit is wild!"

But all of a sudden a man wearing a cowboy outfit, including spurs and a Stetson hat, walked onto the center of the floor. "I say if the little lady wants more, we give her more!"

The audience started clapping wildly.

"You sure you want more, little lady?" the cowboy asked 38DD.

"Yes, I want more," 38DD answered. "I need more. I said it before, and I'll say it again, my pussy is hungry tonight."

"You sure you can handle what I got for you?" the cowboy asked.

"I can handle anything!"

"You sure you're not going to change your mind?" cowboy asked.

"Just give it me, please!" 38DD answered. "I want more!"

"Well, little lady. I got just what you need. I'll be right back."

A few minutes later, Chastity heard a horse's whinny. Her head and everyone else's swung to the source of the sound, and to her shock she saw the cowboy coming from the back of the basement leading a large pony.

"Oh shit," someone in the crowd said. "You've got to be kidding. She might want more, but I know she don't want all of that."

"She's a freak. I bet she can take it," someone else answered.

The cowboy led the pony onto the floor, and Chastity could see that someone had done some kind of

foreplay, because the pony's dick was already unsheathed and hung at least twenty-two inches, and looked like it was about 12 inches in thickness. And it appeared to be as stiff as a board.

"She try to take that shit in her pussy and it's gonna come out her mouth," someone close to Chastity said. She turned to find Jackie at her side.

"I think this part of the show is some kind of joke," she whispered to Jackie. "There's no way she's gonna be able to handle all of that. It'll tear up her insides."

They could hear other people around them placing bets on whether 38DD was going to be able to get all of the pony inside of her without croaking in the process.

Chastity shook her head. "I don't think I can watch this," she told Jackie. "This is just too wild for me."

Jackie nodded. "Same here. Except this shit is too wild for me to miss. My panties are soaking wet."

"God, I'm glad you said that," Chastity said with a giggle. "Cause I didn't want to admit it, but mine are too."

They watched in silence as men scurried around the center of the floor, carrying two contraptions. One was a long metal slat with two slots into which they inserted the pony's front hooves, then strapped them in. The other metal slat they actually screwed into the floor, and then inserted the pony's back hooves, again strapping them in.

"Look at how the pony's acting," Jackie said. "It don't even seem interested in what's goin' on. You think it's drugged?"

Chastity nodded. "Yeah, they probably gave it some kind of tranquilizer."

The pony gave a soft whinny as one of the men pushed a button on the side of the front contraption, and it slowly rose up until the pony's feet were three feet in the air.

The men, then placed what looked like a motorized metal bench press under the pony, and helped 38DD onto the bench. The red head pushed a button on the side of the bench, and it rose up until the woman's body was almost touching the pony's stomach. She then pressed another button, and the bench slid forward then back.

"Okay," the cowboy shouted. "You sure you can handle all this meat?"

"Yeah," 38DD shouted back. "My pussy is hungry for all the meat it can get."

The red head dipped her hand into a bucket of grease someone had placed on the floor, and started slathering it onto the pony's dick, then onto to 38DD's pussy crack.

"This is your last chance to back out," the cowboy shouted.

"Gimme the dick! I want the dick!" 38DD shouted in response.

"Are you sure wanna watch this?" Jackie asked in a husky voice.

"No, but I can't bring myself to look away," Chastity said, as she tried to control her heavy breathing, and also ignore the increasing moisture in her underwear. She looked around the room. Every man in sight had an erection straining against the front of the pants, trying to break free. She and Jackie weren't the only ones turned on. She scanned the room for Legend,

but couldn't find him. A sudden chorus of "ooh," forced her attention back to the pony show. Two men were holding 38DD's legs up in the air, forming a vee, and the red head had the pony's dick in her hand and was rubbing it against 38DD's crack. The motorized bench was far enough away from the pony so that only about two inches of the pony's dick could reach 38DD's pussy.

"Go ahead and put it in her pussy," someone shouted.

"Better yet, put it in her ass," someone else shouted, causing the rest of the audience to laugh.

38DD and the red head joined in the laughter, but once quiet had once again been obtained, the red head pressed the pony's dick against 38DD's pussy and slowly began forcing it in – no easy task since the pony's dick was so thick around.

"Shit, I'm about to bust a nut," a man in the audience said. Chastity looked around and saw that almost half the men were rubbing their dicks through their pants.

38DD let out a small groan as the tip of the head finally entered her, and the red head paused to ask her if she was okay. When 38DD nodded, the red head started pushing again, and soon the head of the pony's dick was inserted inside of her. 38DD's face was twisted into a grimace, and she was breathing hard – Chastity guessed it was more from pain then passion, but after about a minute 38DD tapped the red head's arm, and on the red head obligingly pushed another inch into the woman. Red head then paused, but the pony suddenly seemed to come to life, and it thrust another two inches inside, and probably would have pushed even more if his dick could have reached. 38DD let out a small scream, and the audience let out a gasp, and the red head quickly reached

down to hit the button that would push the bench back away from the pony, but the cowboy stopped her.

"She's okay. Aren't you, little darling?"

38DD bit her lip, and looked up at him and nodded quickly. "Just gotta catch my breath," she said weakly. She continued to breathe heavily, but after two minutes, she gave the red head a nod, and the woman pushed the button which moved the bench toward, then away, from the pony's body, allowing an inch or so more in each time.

"Look at that shit," Chastity said. "You can actually see the outline of that horse dick inside her. It looks like it's gonna bust out her stomach."

"Yeah, but the shit that got's me fucked up is that the bitch is actually starting to act like she likes it."

It was true. 38DD's moans had turned from those of pain to unmistakable pleasure. And even the red head had one hand between her legs playing with herself while operating the button with the other. As for the pony, the tranquilizer must have at least partially worn off, because he was straining to control his own dick movements, though he was still unable to do so because of the metal restraints. Still he snorted and panted like any man getting his brains fucked out.

Red head was moving the bench back and forth faster now, and 38DD was gyrating her hips and twisting her head back and forth in what looked like ecstasy. She was easily taking in more than half the pony's length by this time, and was rubbing her breasts with one hand, and playing with her clitoris with the other.

"I'm ready. Fuck it, I'm ready," she shouted to the red head. "Give me all of it."

The crowd started cheering, and when the redhead looked at the cowboy he hesitated but then

RAW

nodded his head. The red head let the bench slide forward, though she decreased the speed, until 38DD had the pony's dick inside her to the hilt. The audience started cheering, and really went wild when 38DD started lifting her hips up from the bench and shouted shouting, "Let him fuck me. Let him fuck me." The cowboy started chuckling, and gave the red head a nod. She then started sliding the bench back and forward, at an ever increasing speed.

"Oh, God, I'm about to cum," 38DD screamed as she was continually slamming into the pony's dick. "I'm going to cum!"

Chastity turned to Jackie. "The girl licking her didn't make her cum; the champagne bottle didn't make her cum; and that big ass dick on the man didn't make her cum, but now she's getting ready to cum by fucking a horse?"

"Girl, I can't say shit, because I'm about to cum, too."

No sooner were the words out Jackie's mouth than the pony let out a series of loud snorts, and 38DD let out a scream of pure pleasure. The red head had finally stopped moving the bench back and forth, and as 38DD lay still on the bench, her eyes closed and a look of pure satisfaction appeared on her face as what seemed like a gallon of horse sperm spilled out of her pussy. Damn if the 38DD and the pony hadn't come at the same time.

"Now see," Jackie said, when she was finally able to collect herself enough to speak. "That's what you call a freak."

47

Chapter Three

It took a minute for Chastity to remember where she was, and how she'd gotten there, but then the events of the night before came flooding back. Oh, yeah, she said looking around at the room, she was in Legend's residential brownstone, next door to the party house, in the third floor guestroom, and Jackie was in the second floor spare room. Both she and Jackie had crashed there since Legend insisted she was too tired too drive – the party hadn't broken up until dawn. She looked at the clock on the night table next to the bed. It was almost one in the afternoon.

She got up and stretched, wondering where Legend was, and if she could talk him into taking her and Jackie out for brunch. She didn't have to wonder long.

"Yo, princess, you up?" a voice said after a quick three taps on the bedroom door. "Ready to get your grub on?"

Chastity smiled. Gone was the perfect diction and vernacular of the night before that Legend used when around his monied guests. This was the Legend she had come to know and love.

"Come on in, handsome," she yelled through the door.

Legend's hair was loose, and brushing his shoulders. And since he was also shirtless and barefoot, Chastity found it hard to tear her eyes away from his

chiseled and bulging biceps. "How long have you been up?" she asked, trying to bring herself to some kind of semblance of composure.

Legend chuckled, rubbing his hand over his massive chest as he sat down on the edge of her bed. "Up? I ain't been down yet. I had to count up all that paper we made last night."

"Oh man, Legend," Chastity threw off the sheet and scrambled over to sit by him. The sleeves of the shirt Legend had loaned her to sleep in tumbled down over her hands, and she rolled them back up quickly, "I know you cleaned up. That was one helluva party."

"Hell, yeah, ma. That's why it was such short notice. When I found out that freak was in town I hurried up and booked her. I seen her do her thing at a private party in Las Vegas, so I knew she'd be a goldmine. I had hell getting that damn pony into the basement, though."

"Yeah, I was wondering how the hell you did that."

"I left it to them," Legend said casually. "But they know their shit. They brought the pony up in one of them little horse trailers attached to a car, then they blindfolded the pony, put one of them wooden planks on the basement steps, and led him down." He gave a little laugh. "So then I hurried up and put the word out on the street and let my usual guests know that we had something special. So special they had to pay double to get in."

"Double?" Chastity's eyes widened.

"Yep, you got two thousand coming to you from the table, instead of your usual one thousand. And your take on the coke and pills comes up to another five hundred."

Chastity frowned. "Legend, you know I don't want –"

Legend put his hand up. "Stop it, Chas. You know how I feel about that shit. You do a job, you get paid. That was the deal in the beginning between me and you, and it's gonna be the deal until the end. Professional all the way."

Chastity lowered her eyes and bit her lip. She had come, so many times in the past three years, to regret her words he now echoed back to her.

"You shoulda seen Jackie when I told her she's getting double," Legend said, either not noticing or ignoring Chastity's sudden change in mood. "She started jumping up and down and shouting so loud the dog next door started barking. Next time I'ma make her ass sleep in the basement where I got soundproofing."

"Yeah," Chastity said. "So she wound up getting a thousand for the night instead of the two fifty she thought she was going to get for the party. By the way, how'd she do as a diva?"

Legend shook his head. "I gotta give it to the girl, she did a helluva job. The word I got back from her guests was that she was crude, but charming. Now, see, that crude shit ain't no way fucking charming to me, but some niggas like it. I'm going to let her host the five hundred dollar tables a few more times, and maybe eventually move her up to a seven-fifty. She might be a money-maker after all."

"See? I told you," Chastity said triumphantly. "You always did underestimate Jackie."

Legend shrugged his massive shoulders. "Yeah, at first, maybe. But she's definitely grown on me. I like the way she's always been a good friend to you. Always

in your corner. Just that alone is enough to make me like her."

Chastity gave him a hug. "I don't know what I would have done without Jackie, and without you."

Legend smiled. "Yeah, well. You've done pretty damn well on your own, girl. You're the real money-maker. Now if I could convince you to enroll your pretty ass in school I'd consider my life work done."

Chastity shrugged and moved away a little. "Not that again."

"Damn, Chas," Legend shook his head. "As smart as you are, there just ain't no reason to –"

"Come on, now, Legend," Chastity cut him off, "We've been over this before. I need to be out here making money. I don't have time to go to school yet. But I will. I promise."

"I've told you before I'll pay your tuition, Chas."

"But I've also got to pay lawyers."

"And you think I can't afford to take care of that, too? Shit, ma, get in school and I promise I'll pay all your bills."

Chastity sighed. "Yeah, I know you would. But I like taking care of myself. Besides, I don't want to get into college until I know my father will be home to see me graduate. It was his dream more than mine."

"Oh shit." Legend glanced at his watch. "Where's your cell phone?"

"In my bag. Why?"

"Hurry up and get it out for a minute."

"Why?" Chastity said as she opened up the night table drawer and withdrew her iPhone.

"Cause I have a present for you," Legend said simply. "Is it on?"

Shay

Chastity nodded, wondering what Legend was up to.

"Okay, it's going to be exactly one' o'clock in exactly ten, nine, eight, seven, six, five, four, three, two, one –"

As if on cue, her phone started ringing. But when Chastity looked, the number which came up was one she wasn't familiar with. "Who . . ."

"Hurry up and answer," Legend said urgently.

"Hello," she said, looking at Legend skeptically.

"Chastity?" came an all too familiar voice.

"Daddy? Daddy! Oh my God, Daddy!" Chastity jumped off the bed. "How did you . . . I mean, how are you . . . Daddy, how are you able to call me on my cell phone? I mean, this isn't even a collect call!"

"I know, I know," Ronald Jones answered, with a laugh. "God, it's good to hear your voice. And it's not even a Tuesday."

"But how –"

"Well, someone slipped me a cell phone, courtesy of your friend, Legend, girl. Said for me to give you call at exactly one o'clock, and gave me your cell number. So here I am."

"Oh, Daddy! I can't believe . . . oh, this is so great," Chastity looked at Legend, who was still sitting on the side of the bed, grinning. She punched him softly on his shoulder. "Daddy, how are you doing?"

"Same as always, I guess. Keeping my head up, and all that. How are you doing, baby girl?"

"I'm fine, Daddy. I'm keeping my head up, too. I was talking to the lawyer on Thursday, and he said things are going well on your appeal. Did he tell you?"

"Yeah, Gephardt told me. But we'll see. I mean, hell, there ain't no way he's ever gonna be able to get me outta here."

"But at least you'll be alive, Daddy. And that has to mean something," Chastity said. "And once they get the death penalty thrown out, maybe we can figure out something to get you freed."

"Well, I wouldn't count on –"

"Daddy? Daddy!" Chastity looked at her phone. "Oh, hell, I ran out of juice!"

"You've got to be kidding," Legend took the phone away from her and looked at it. "Damn, girl. You need to do a better job keeping your phone charged."

"If I had known I was going to be staying over I would have brought my charger," Chastity whined.

Legend sighed. "I'm sorry."

"Why?" Chastity said, wiping a tear from her eye.

"If I had let you drive home last night your phone woulda been charged, and you could have talked longer. I was being selfish. I wanted to see your face when you got the phone call."

Chastity sighed. "Don't worry about it. Let me borrow your cell so I can call him back."

Legend shook his head. "No, princess, it doesn't work like that. You can't ever call him because the guards might hear the phone. Your old man'll get thrown in the hole if they find out he has a cell phone."

"Oh." She sat thinking for a minute, then said slowly, "But then aren't you putting him at risk by getting him the phone?"

"No, not really. Not if he follows the instructions he's been given," Legend said. "My cousin has one of the guards up there on his payroll. By now

Shay

your father should have passed the phone to another inmate, and he'll be securing it in a safe place. At a designated time every day – or every other day, whatever your choice – the guard will take the inmate and your dad to a secure corner of the stock room, and the inmate will pass him the phone. Then when your dad is finished he'll just give the phone back to the inmate."

"But won't the other inmate get in trouble if they search his cell and find the phone?"

"He doesn't have it secured in his cell."

Chastity frowned. "Well, then where does he keep it?"

Legend chuckled. "Don't ask."

"Why? I mean . . . " Her eyes widened and she started laughing. "Ooh, that's so nasty."

"Uh huh. But you gotta do what you gotta do."

Chastity moved closer to Legend, and placed her head on his shoulder. "Thanks, Legend. You really look out for me, and for my father. I really appreciate it."

"Don't mention it, princess," he said rubbing her back. "You know I'll always do whatever I can for you."

She nestled closer, savoring the smell of his cologne, and the hardness of his body, and wishing she could turn back the hands of time so she could really feel it, and not just his shoulders and his chest, but his rippled stomach as he lay on top of her, driving her crazy as he moved back and forth inside of her. There was no man who ever made her feel the way she knew Legend did. And she knew that if they made love it would be complete love making, not just sex. They would be one, physically, mentally, and emotionally. No man had ever made her feel that way. No man ever will, she thought sadly, as her eyes filled with tears.

"Damn," Legend said suddenly.

"What's wrong?" Chastity's head jerked up and she looked at him.

"I just thought of something. What would happen if they forgot to turn the phone off before the other inmate, um, secured it, and you just happened to call the phone while he was on the chow line or something." Legend threw his head back and started laughing uproariously. "That would be one musical-ass nigga."

Chastity looked at him, and screwed up her face. "You are so nasty!"

"Yeah," Legend leaned down and kissed her on the forehead. "But that's why you love me."

If only you knew, Chastity thought as Legend got up and exited the room. *If only you knew.*

"I'm telling ya, ain't shit to this. All you gotta do is dance, and take off your clothes to the music," Jackie said as she and Chastity shared a blunt inside the storage space which doubled as the dancer's dressing room in the bar on 143rd Street. There were five or six other girls in the storage space, but they ignored the two girls. Chastity figured they must not like Jackie. Which wasn't unusual, Jackie was never good at making friends with other females. In fact, Chastity was the only girlfriend she had.

"Ya don't even have to look at none of them niggas in the crowd, if you 'on't wanna," she continued. "But I'ma tell ya, ya can make a lot more money if you do. At least if you give the eye to the right nigga," she added with a grin.

Shay

Chastity shivered, rubbing her hands over her arms, trying to make the goose bumps disappear. "But none of them are supposed to touch me, right?"

"They ain't supposed to, 'cept when they puttin' money in your G-string," Jackie explained, as she popped an ecstasy pill in her mouth, then washed it down with a swig of beer. "But I don't complain if they push down it a little further then they 'spose to if it's a Grant or a C-note; 'course with these cheap ass niggas in this funky spot that don't happen too often."

Chastity nodded. It was her first night dancin', but she'd been up front watching the other girls, including Jackie, do their thing. Technically, it didn't look hard. She loved to dance and had taken two years of ballet at the neighborhood community center; she knew she could move better than anyone she'd seen out there, including Jackie. Emotionally, though, she was fucked up. The thought of men leering at her the way James did that night . . . she shivered again.

She had called Jackie on her cell phone on her way back to Harlem after leaving Queens, and the girl had met her at the subway station and then smuggled her into her bedroom. Chastity had hid in the closet the next morning while everyone was getting ready for school and work. Jackie had dawdled, making sure she was the last one to leave, then doubled back to the apartment 15 minutes later, after making sure the coast was clear.

Chastity had told Jackie the night before that she wanted to go to school, but Jackie had reasoned with her that if she did, the police – or worse, the foster care people – might be there ready to pick her up if Miss Daisy had called to say she was missing. It took them almost a week of trying to come up with ideas, but the two had decided that the only thing to do was to go

56

RAW

through with their original plan. Jackie had already
started dancing at the illegal men's only club –
appropriately named The Meat Club – a few weeks
before, and said she was clearing between two and three
hundred dollars a night, and her wardrobe attested to the
fact. Gone were the American Eagle and Gap jeans that
had dominated Jackie's closet when Chastity was there a
month before; replaced by True Religion's and Citizens,
which cost $150 and up. She also had an assortment of
Coach bags, and all sorts of gold jewelry.

"I'm tellin' ya," Jackie had said, "Between the
two of us we can get the money up for an apartment up
in no time. I bet we have our own place in like a month."

Chastity nodded. Though she'd only been there
three days, she was ready to move out the room she'd
rented from a woman – Miss Cindy – who let out rooms
in her 3-bedroom apartment in the Lincoln Projects. The
place was swarming with roaches, which wasn't
surprising since Miss Cindy and her three sons were
nasty slobs. Raggedy and smelly people knocked on the
door all times of night, courtesy of the fact that two of
Miss Cindy sons were dealing crack. And Miss Cindy
would get drunk at least five nights a week and blast
Whitney Houston's *I Will Always Love You* so loud the
walls would quake. Still beggars, couldn't be choosers,
and there weren't many places a 16-year-old could find
housing with no questions asked.

"Okay, you're 'bout to be up," Jackie said,
taking another swig of her beer. "You gonna be ai'ght?"

"Yeah, yeah, I'll be fine." Chastity stood up,
then took a deep breath and looked in the cracked dirty
mirror someone had glued to the wall in the corner of the
storage room. She barely recognized the girl reflected
back in the glass. The red negligee she wore was cut so

57

low it barely covered her ample breasts, and so low her butt cheeks were visible. Her lipstick was fire engine red, which matched her negligee but did nothing for her light bronze complexion, nor did the heavy red blush and jet-black mascara. If she was going to stick with this job she was going to have to bring her own make-up rather than rely what they had at the club. She grimaced. She looked like a damn kewpie doll, though she knew the club wanted her to have a China Doll look.

"You look great, girl," Jackie said, as if reading her thoughts. "Now go on out and shake them big tits and fat ass."

Chastity didn't look back. As the opening strains of R. Kelly's latest slow jam started playing, she leisurely sauntered out. She hadn't even gotten to the middle of the stage before the hoots and hollas began.

"Look at that big titty China Doll," one drunk shouted. "We gonna see some real shit tonight."

Taking a deep breath, and trying to ignore the shouts and whistles, Chastity began swaying to the music, moving her shoulders sexily, and running her hands through her hair, over her breasts, and then down to her crotch area, slowly rubbing the material of the negligee so that it rode up, revealing her thong while the crowd roared its approval.

She lazily licked her lips, and then let her head fall back as if she were in a state of rapture, swaying her hips in time to the music while still rubbing herself through the negligee.

"Take it off! Show us whatchoo workin' wiff," someone shouted.

In answer, Chastity turned around, then slowly bent down – keeping up with the slow tempo of the song – so that her ass was in perfect view, and then reached

between her legs and slowly fingered her thong from front to back. Again, the crowd responded with an approving roar.

She turned back to face the audience, and started dancing a little faster, still rubbing her breasts and crotch area. Her plan had been to ease the negligee's spaghetti straps over her shoulders, as she'd seen the other girls do, but instead, when the song hit a dramatic drum beat, she suddenly ripped the negligee down the middle, and held the torn sides open wide to reveal her heaving sweaty breasts. The reaction was just what she had hoped for; she stood there just quivering her body to the music as men stood up on chairs shouting and applauding. After a minute or so she started swaying again, and then did a couple of deliberate spins, letting the torn negligee fall to the stage floor. She then did a slow split, rubbing her breasts as her body eased down to the floor. She then arched her back, and brought her foot up to touch her head.

"Damn! That bitch must be double-jointed," she heard someone shout.

Not double-jointed, just talented. As the song droned to an end, she twisted her torso to face the crowd, then swung her legs forward so they were straight in front of her. She then eased herself up and out of the split, and when she was standing in front of them, wearing nothing but her thong and still swaying her hips and shoulders to the music, she stuck her hand deep inside her thong, swirled it around, then trailed it up her body, between her breasts, over her throat, and then brought her index finger to her mouth and gave it a languid lick. She then kissed the finger, pointed it at the crowd, and blew a kiss.

Shay

"Let's hear a big round applause for China Doll," the emcee said as he walked on the stage. "Is she wonderful or what?"

Chastity smiled, bowed, and then walked off the stage and into the crowd as the DJ put on the six-minute version of Lil Wayne's latest single. The beat was fast, which pleased her as she wiggled her shoulders and hips to the beat, pausing at tables that waved her over if the men held dollar bills in their hands. She followed Jackie's advice, and let the men with tens and twenties get a deeper and longer feel then the ones who gave up fives, and even treated them to a quick shoulder rub, and a kiss on the forehead. For the men who were only stuffing ones she simply flashed a smile.

As the song came to the end, and she was dancing her way backstage she bumped into a tall man in a white suit whose back was turned to her. When he turned to face her she quickly inhaled. He wasn't just handsome, he wasn't just fine, he was the shit; long black hair that hung on his shoulders, a reddish copper complexion, and dark piercing eyes that looked deep into hers as he spoke.

"You're pretty good, ma," he said in a soft baritone voice that she had to strain to hear over the music. "Very good, in fact. How long have you been dancing?"

She looked at him, and shook her head, causing him to frown.

"What exactly does that mean?" he asked.

She just shook her head again. He gave her a puzzled look, then reached into his pocket and pulled out a platinum business card holder. "Okay, if and when you decide to speak, give me a call."

She took the card he handed her, and slid it down her body as if to put it in her pocket, then remembered she didn't have a pocket. Shit, she didn't have on any clothes. She did the next best thing, she slid it in her thong.

He looked at her and smiled, revealing a set of pearly white teeth which were so perfect they almost looked fake. "Wait," he said, pulling out a platinum money clip that matched the business card holder. "I think this is what you need to be putting down that G-string." He counted out five one-hundred dollar bills, put it in her hand rather than her thong, and then walked away.

"Girl, you had 'em goin' out there," Jackie said when she finally made it backstage. "I know you cleaned up, ho. And was that who I thought it was speakin' to just now?"

"Huh?" Chastity asked as she sat down on one of the boxes, ignoring the other girls, most of whom were putting on their street clothes and getting ready to go home.

"Who was that guy you was speakin' to?" Jackie said impatiently.

"I don't know, but he was fine, wasn't he?" Chastity said. She pulled the business card out of her thong and gave it to Jackie. "But he gave me his card."

"Oh Good Goddamn!" Jackie almost shouted when she read it. "I thought that nigga was Legend. Shit, I been tryin' to meet up with him for more than a minute now. And you just get up in here and he's talkin' to you your first night. Shit, if you wasn't my girl I'd be jealous. So what was y'all talkin' 'bout?"

"He asked me how long I'd been dancing."

"Yeah? You tell him this was your first night?"

Chastity shook her head.

"No? What you tell him?"

Chastity blushed. "Um, actually, I didn't say anything."

"What do you mean?"

Chastity giggled. "I was so busy looking at him that I couldn't speak. I mean, damn, you seen his eyes? They were like . . . like he was some kind of hypnotist or something."

Jackie's mouth dropped open. "So you ain't answer him? You ain't say shit?"

"No, I was –"

"Damn, bitch. You stupid or something? You know who that nigga Legend is? That nigga is made of money. You shoulda been all up his shit. I know I woulda been. Damn." Jackie gave a scathing look. "You so busy lookin' at his eyes, you ain't notice that ice on his fingers? And I heard he rocks a 2006 silver Benz."

"Well, I didn't know all that, but I figured he must have some dough. Look at the tip he gave me." Chastity opened her fist and smoothed out the bills he'd slipped her.

Jackie's eyes widened. "Five hundred dollars? Aw shit now. That's what the fuck I'm talkin' 'bout. He's on you!"

A skinny dark-skinned girl with a rainbow Afro wig that looked like a leftover from a 70's blaxploitation movie scooted over to Chastity's side. "Did I hear you say you got a $500 tip? You lyin', right?"

"Naw, my girl ain't gotta lie about her shit," Jackie said, putting her arm around Chastity protectively. "And anyway, ain't no one was talkin' to you, Tamika. What you doin' tryin' to get all in our business?"

The girl stood there for a moment, looking Jackie up and down as if deciding whether or not to try her. She finally sucked her teeth. "Well, fuck you then," she said over her shoulder as she walked away.

"You gotta watch these jealous bitches in here," Jackie said loud enough for Tamika to hear. "They all be hatin'."

"Forget her," Chastity said as she counted the other money that had been stuffed down her thong. "With what that guy Legend gave me, I think I made about eight hundred dollars."

"Aw yeah, that's what's up." Jackie rubbed her hands together. "You keep this shit up we gonna be able to get that apartment next week instead of next month."

Chastity waited until she and Jackie were in a cab on the way home before she brought up Legend again. "So, tell me about him. How does he make his money? He only looks like he's about twenty-five or something. Is he dealing?"

"Yeah, I think so. I mean, I guess in a way, you know," Jackie answered. "I don't know him personally, but from what I understand he deals, but only to his private customers."

"What do you mean?"

"Well, the nigga is rich because he gives these hot parties everybody wants to go to, but they're invitation only. Bunch of basketball and football players be up in there, and rap stars and movie people and shit. You know celebrities. They know they can go to his parties and don't have to worry 'bout what they do gettin' in the papers so they can get their freak on."

Chastity frowned. "So how does he keep money if he's always throwing it away giving these parties?"

Shay

Jackie shook her head. "You don't get it. The parties is how he makes his shit. He charges like a $200 cover charge, and there's a cash bar. But," her voice suddenly took on an excited tone, "from what I hear, the thing is that's just for the upstairs parties."

"What do you mean?"

"Well, the word is that while people are partyin' upstairs, there's another party goin' on downstairs. And niggas be giving up the big bucks to get down there. Like $500 and up."

Chastity's head jerked back. "Get outta here!"

Jackie nodded. "I hear he pays girls to give sex shows, and shit for entertainment. That's the party I'm tryin' to get into."

"Girl, I know you're not thinking about doing a sex show!"

Jackie sucked her teeth. "Get the fuck outta here. No, bitch. But he also pays girls to come to his parties and help keep the party goin'. You know, profile, dance a little – with their clothes on – and just keep it live. Encourage the niggas to keep buying drinks, and shit. That's why I been tryin' to get up with him. To see if he'll ask me to come to one of his parties. You get $200 just for coming, and the tips are like triple what we usually get at The Meat Club. From what I hear he goes to different nightclubs and spots like ours to see the new blood out there." Jackie crossed her arms over her chest. "Damn, he musta come after I did my thing tonight. Else I bet he woulda put me on."

Chastity's breath caught in her throat. "Jackie, you think he gave me his card and told me to call because he wants me for one of his parties?"

"Aw hell, yeah," Jackie said confidently. "And you betta jump on it, too. And you betta make sure you get me in with you."

"Hell yeah." The two girls gave each a high five.

It wasn't until later that night, as she was getting undressed for bed, that Chastity realized she no longer had the card. "I must have dropped it in the storage room," she told Jackie the next morning. The two wasted no time hopping in a cab and dashing over to The Meat Club, but even though they searched the storage space from top to bottom they couldn't find the business card.

"I bet that bitch Tamika swiped it," Jackie huffed. "I oughtta slide that bitch."

"What are we going to do now?" Chastity wailed. "Do you think you can get his number from someone?"

"Shit, if I coulda got his number I woulda been called him," Jackie said. "I told you I been tryin' to get with him. Fuck, I thought you was gonna be my ticket in, Chas."

It was another two months before Chastity ran into Legend again. She and Jackie were just walking in The Meat Club, heading for the dressing room, when she saw him at the bar talking to the club manager. She elbowed Jackie, "Look who's here!"

"Aw shit, now. Here's our chance," Jackie whispered. "And don't get choked up and not talk to him this time. Fuck his eyes. And I mean that shit."

"Don't worry. I got this covered," Chastity answered as she walked over and took a seat at the bar next to Legend. His back was to her as he continued talking to the manager. They were talking too low for her to hear what they were saying, but just the melodious tone of his baritone made her feel warm and tingly

inside. *I've got to keep myself together,* she warned herself. *I can't let him think that I'm some dumb girl. I gotta come off cool.* She reached inside her pocketbook and pulled out a breath mint and popped it in her mouth while waiting for him to turn around and notice her. She could have sworn that he glanced in the mirror over the bar and saw her, but he still didn't turn around. She began to feel nervous, and to make matters worse, she had to go to the bathroom. She waited another five minutes, then slid off the barstool after she was afraid her bladder was going to burst. Jackie, who had taken a seat in one of the booths near the corner of the club hurried after her as she strode into the ladies room.

"Girl, will you hurry up? You want him to leave?" Jackie shouted as Chastity relieved herself.

"I'm hurrying, I'm hurrying," Chastity answered as she tore off a piece of toilet paper. "But I'm getting the feeling he doesn't want to talk to me."

"Why you say that?"

"Damn, Jackie. I sat there for ten minutes and he never even turned around." Chastity came out the stall and washed her hands.

They emerged from the ladies room just in time to see Legend stand up, and shake the manager's hand.

"Shit," Jackie exclaimed. "He's gettin' ready to split!" She gave Chastity a shove forward, almost knocking her off her feet. Chastity regained her balance, shot Jackie a dirty look, then strode over past the bar, purposely bumping into Legend's arm.

"Oh, I'm so sorry," she said quickly. She was mortified when she realized that he had been holding a drink, and she had caused it to spill on his suit jacket. "Oh, I'm really sorry."

Legend looked at her quizzically while reaching for a napkin from the bar. "That's alright, don't even worry about it." He dabbed at the spreading spot on his jacket. "Good to find out you can talk, though. I was beginning to think you were dumb or something."

"Dumb?" Chastity's embarrassment turned into a quick flash of anger. "What do you mean dumb?"

"Cool out," Legend said, flashing that pearly white smile. "Dumb as in mute. You know, like deaf, dumb and blind. Get it now?" He laughed, and Chastity found herself joining in.

"So, all right," Legend said after an awkward moment of silence. "I gotta roll. Catch you lata."

"Wait!" Chastity said as he strode from the bar.

"What?" he asked turning around, raising one of his eyebrows as he did.

"I was just –" Chastity's mind raced, trying to figure out something to say to keep the conversation going. "Well, I just wanted to pay for you to get that suit cleaned."

Legend glanced down at the spot and waved his hand dismissively. "Like I said, don't worry about it."

"But it's such a nice suit," Chastity said, walking over to him. She touched the jacket lightly. "And it looks so expensive."

Legend cocked his head to the side and gave her a funny look. "Yeah, huh?"

"Yeah. And, I mean, I bet it cost at least a couple of hundred dollars."

"Is that right?"

Legend's stare was so intense Chastity found herself blushing. "I mean, yeah," she stammered. "I know I couldn't afford to buy you a new one with what I make here, but I can at least offer to get it cleaned."

Shay

Legend crossed his arms. "So," he said slowly. "Why are you so talkative today when you never even bothered to call after I gave you my number?"

"I lost it! I really did. I mean, I know that sounds like a line, but I really did," Chastity said all in a rush. "You can ask my girlfriend." She turned and scanned the club for Jackie, then motioned her to come over.

"Jackie, what did I say happened to Legend's number? Tell him," Chastity said urgently.

"Well, you said, uh –"

"No, for real. Tell him the truth," Chastity urged.

Jackie gave her a "for real?" look, and waited for Chastity to nod before saying, "Well, she lost it. She thought she left it in the storage, uh, the dressing room, and we even went back and looked for it, but we couldn't find it."

"See?" Chastity said triumphantly. "I told you."

Legend shook his head. "Why are you tripping? I didn't ask for a witness, now did I?"

"No, but I –"

Legend gave a snort, and the look of disgust on his face was unmistakable. Chastity's heart sank as she wondered exactly what she'd done wrong. She looked at Jackie for help, but her friend just gave a short shrug.

"Okay," Chastity said, her eyes glued to the floor in embarrassment. "Well, I guess if you've gotta go –"

"You working tonight?" Legend asked suddenly.

"Yes, I –"

"Yeah she is," Jackie broke in. "I am, too. You know you just oughtta stick around and see our sets."

"Hmph, well, tell your manager your friend's taking the night off. She's having dinner with me,"

Legend said abruptly. "And I'll stop by and check you out another time." He looked at Chastity. "Come on."

Jackie had heard wrong; he didn't have a silver Benz, he had a silver Jaguar. He used the keyless remote to unlock the doors, and Chastity quickly climbed in the passenger seat. She couldn't resist running her hand over the smooth as butter leather seats before buckling herself in. Now this is a car, she thought, as Legend stuck his key in the ignition and took off down the street. He didn't say anything during the ride, so she didn't either, satisfying herself looking out the window and speculating as to where he was taking her to eat. She figured it was going to be some place nice, though. The man obviously had style. Damn, she thought, I hope it's someplace that lets you wear jeans.

"Here we are," Legend said as he pulled into a parking lot. "I hope you like seafood."

"Is it okay that I'm wearing jeans?" she asked as she looked out the window at the expensive looking restaurant situated on a river dock.

"It's fine. I'm just glad you're not wearing sneakers," Legend said with a grin as he opened his car door. "But for real, girl, it's all good. I'm a regular here, so it wouldn't be a problem anyway."

Chastity climbed out the car, and was pleasantly surprised when Legend offered her his arm to lead her inside the restaurant. He'd taken off his stained suit jacket, and had flung it over his shoulder.

"Mr. Spicer, good to see you this evening," the maître d' said when they reached the podium.

"Thank you. We'd like a table on the perimeter if one is open," Legend answered.

He waited until they were seated, the menus were placed in front of them, and the host had left before

smiling pleasantly at Chastity and saying, "So, tell me something good, ma."

"Like what?" she asked.

"Well, for starters, what's your name?"

"My . . . Oh my God, I haven't even told you my name." Chastity started laughing. "I didn't even realize it."

"Yeah, well I did." Legend grinned. "The first time I spoke you ain't open your mouth. And then when you finally decided to speak tonight all you did was try to run game. What's up with that?"

"Run game? I wasn't trying to run any –"

"Oh, that's such an expensive suit," Legend said in a high falsetto voice. "It must have cost a couple hundred dollars."

Chastity blushed as he echoed her words. "I was just –"

"I know I couldn't afford to buy you a new one," Legend continued in the falsetto, while batting his eyes, "at least with what I make here." Legend started laughing, and then said in his normal baritone, "Either go ahead and say it is what you want, or learn how to make your hints more subtle."

Chastity's eyes fell to the table. "So, did you bring me all the way out here to make me feel bad?"

"Naw, I brought you all the way out to here to find out your name." Legend placed his hand over hers. "Stop acting all embarrassed. I'm just teasing."

"Chastity. My name is Chastity."

"Chastity what?"

"Chastity Jones."

"Nice to meet you, Chastity." Legend patted her hand. "Now, how old are you?"

"Sixteen. I'll be seventeen in a few weeks."

RAW

"Really?" Legend's eyebrow shot up. "I would have thought you were older than that."

"I know. That's because I carry myself with class."

"Oh?" Legend took a sip of his water and looked at her strangely. "Actually, I thought you were older because of the way you look. What are you about 5'10? Most teenagers that tall are still kind of skinny and underdeveloped. But you are certainly filled out like a grown woman. And you sure as hell dance like a grown woman. I saw that the other night."

Chastity blushed again, hating herself for doing so. There was nothing lewd or rude about the way he made his comment, it was definitely meant as a compliment and she took it as such. But she couldn't help it. There was something about him that made her feel a little star struck.

"So how long have you been dancing?"

"That night you saw me at the club was my first night?"

"Get outta here. You handled yourself like a pro."

"Thanks," Chastity mumbled.

"So . . . tell me a little more about yourself, shortie. Where are you from? Here in New York?"

Chastity nodded. "Right in Harlem. Born and raised on 132nd and St. Nicholas. Near the Lionel Hampton's. I don't live there anymore, though. Jackie, my . . . uh . . . witness back at the club, and I have an apartment now on 149th and Adam Clayton Powell Blvd."

"The Dunbar Apartments?"

"Yeah. We're subletting a two-bedroom. It's small, but it's okay. And the rent is reasonable. We're

71

going to get a bigger and better apartment when we save more money."

"You two must be close."

"Very. We've known each other since first grade. We used to live in the same building on 132nd Street. Went to the same elementary school, were in the same classes. We've always been best friends."

He was easy to talk to, and he asked just enough questions to let her know he was really interested in what she was saying. Over dinner, and then dessert she spilled out almost her entire life story; including her mother's infidelity, her father's incarceration, and her brief stint in foster care, and having to drop out of high school. But though she told him that she'd run away from the foster home, she didn't tell him why. She'd never even told Jackie.

"Damn, ma. You've been through some tough shit," Legend said sympathetically when she was through. "So that's how you wound up dancing at The Meat Club, huh? That's some real tough shit." Then he paused. "Hunter High, huh? That's one of the best schools in the city. You've been there since the eighth grade? I guess that's why you're so articulate."

"Yeah, I guess. And my father was big on me using proper English. A lot of the kids around the block used to tease me and say I talk like a white girl."

Legend grimaced. "That shows their ignorance. That's an insult to black folks. Speaking proper English doesn't mean you speak like a white girl. Shit, the white girls raised in ghettos like Hell's Kitchen don't use proper English."

"Yeah, but try telling the kids on the block that," Chastity laughed.

Legend smiled. "You know what, Chastity?"

"What?"

"I love the way you laugh."

Chastity looked down at the table and blushed again.

"No, I really mean it," Legend said, obviously sensing her discomfort. "You have, well, a kind of tingly laugh. Like little bells chiming. It's cute."

Chastity started chewing her lip. "You'd better stop. You keep making me blush."

"Why? Aren't you used to flattering remarks? I know you've musta heard a hundred of them as gorgeous as you are."

Chastity shrugged. "Yeah, but I think you mean yours. Most of the guys who compliment me are only, you know, trying to –"

"Get in your pants?"

"Well, yeah." Chastity squirmed in her seat.

"Yeah, I know how it is. Niggas be niggas. You can't blame them, though."

Chastity shrugged, not knowing what else to say.

"So," Legend said slowly, "do you do anything else at The Meat Club besides dance?"

"What do you mean?"

"You know what I mean."

Chastity caught her breath. She knew what he was talking about. A few of the girls at the club – hell, most of them – turned tricks with some of the regular customers to make extra money. And there was a time or two when she'd also spent some time doing some extra entertainment, but who could blame her? The rent on the apartment was $1,500, and then there were cable, electricity, and cell phone bills, not to mention having to buy clothes since most of hers were left behind when she

73

left Miss Daisy's house. And while she usually cleared $350 a night at The Meat Club, she was only allowed to work two nights a week so that the club could keep a full stable of club for rotation. She was picky about the customers she dallied with, but it was still demeaning, and not a subject she wanted to talk about. And not a subject she thought he should have brought up. She looked him directly in the eyes. "I don't see how that's any of your business."

"Good answer." Legend said, signaling the waiter for the check. "But be prepared because I *will* be asking you again."

"You *will* get the same answer."

"We'll see."

"*You'll* see, you mean," Chastity retorted.

"Yeah, alright, ma." Legend stood up after paying the bill with his platinum American Express Card. "You ready?"

Instead of answering, Chastity slid her chair back and stood up, prompting Legend to shake his head with a small frown.

He walked up close to her. "Listen, walk ahead of me as we leave, okay?" he said in a low voice.

"Why?"

"Just because."

Chastity started walking quickly, with Legend on her heels. "Slow down. We're not in a race," he said in her ear.

When they got to the parking lot he waited until they were at the passenger door before he beeped the remote to unlock the car.

"Stop," he said as Chastity reached for the handle to open the door.

She looked around the parking lot in confusion. "What's wrong?"

"Nothing," he said as opened the door for her. She looked at him quizzically them climbed in.

He then walked around the car and got in on the driver's side. Before putting the key in the ignition he turned in his seat to face her. "When you go to a restaurant or club with a man, when the host or hostess shows you to your seat you follow directly behind him, and let the man follow behind you. When you leave the restaurant, you lead the way. Cool?"

"Cool," she said biting her lips uncomfortably, wondering why he was suddenly tripping. Was he embarrassed by the way she acted, she wondered.

"And when you're getting in a car, wait for the man to open the door for you."

"Look, Legend, most of the guys I know don't open doors."

"How do you know? From what I observe you don't give them a chance."

She bristled, she couldn't help herself. "Yeah, well, I don't want to look like a fool waiting for a car door to be opened and the nigga ain't even thinking about it."

Legend patted her hand. "Calm down. I'm trying to be helpful. You said in there you carry yourself with class, Chastity. Well, you don't carry yourself like someone with *no* class, but I wouldn't say you carry yourself with class, either. What I'm trying to do is show how to act like you think you act anyway."

"Oh? So, what? You're trying to be my teacher or some shit?"

"No, I'm trying to be your friend. But there's nothing wrong with friends learning from each other," Legend said patiently.

"Yeah, and what am I supposed to be teaching you?" Chastity snapped.

"Well, right now I'd say you'd be good at teaching someone how to blow a good thing," Legend said, a little irritation now evident in his voice. He turned the key and pulled off.

They drove in silence for a few minutes, before Legend asked, "You want me to drop you off back at your club?"

"If you want," Chastity said, staring stonily ahead.

Legend let out a sigh, "Look, I apologize if I –"

"I'm sorry."

"Come again?"

"I'm sorry," Chastity repeated. "I shouldn't have jumped on you."

"Then why did you?"

Chastity looked down at her hands. "Because you started out making me feel nervous, then you made me feel really good about myself, and then you started making me feel stupid. I'm just confused."

"Damn, ma. I can see how I . . . look I really am sorry." Legend pulled the car over to the curb, then turned to face Chastity again. He picked her hand up from her lap and held it in his. "Listen, when I first saw you up there on the stage, I looked at the way you danced, and thought, 'Now, that's not just a regular dancer. That's a chick with some class.' Then when I tried to speak to you and you froze up, I thought, 'that's a nervous little girl.' And then when you approached me the way did at the club, I thought, 'That's a gold-digger.'

76

And when we went out and got to really talking, I realized you're all of that and more. And it all makes you . . . well it makes you . . . I don't know, it makes you something else."

Chastity chuckled. "Okay, now I'm really confused.

Legend nodded. "Yeah, I'm a little confused myself at the moment. But there are a few things I know for sure. One is that you have a lot of potential, but if you don't work on yourself now, while you're still young, it's only going to be wasted potential. You have some rough edges. Let me help you work on those."

"Well, I –"

"Let me," Legend insisted. "You're a beautiful young girl. So beautiful that no one is going to want to help you reach your full potential. There'll be some guys who will be so happy to be kicking it with a chick like you that they'll just accept you the way you are, and while that sounds nice, that doesn't help you grow. And that's fucked up." He paused. "And then there'll be some guys who'll be glad you don't know what you're worth and won't ever want to help you reach your full potential because they figure that way they can get you on the cheap. And that's even more fucked up."

Chastity winced.

"I don't mean to hurt you," Legend said gently, "I'm just trying to keep it real."

"So, what's the deal with you?" Chastity asked after a moment of thought. "Why would you try to help me reach my . . . what you call . . . my full potential?"

"I'm not sure. One reason, I guess, is that I think you're a sweet girl, and if someone doesn't take you under their wing soon you won't be a sweet girl for long."

Shay

"Damn," Chastity said.

"Still just trying to keep it real," Legend said. "You've already experienced some shitty parts of life, so I know you know what I'm talking about. And I'm not trying to turn you into some damn goody-goody. I'm talking about making you a pro instead of just a ho."

"A pro, huh?" Chastity said thoughtfully. "So, you want me to become a high-class prostitute? And you get a cut of whatever I make?"

Legend looked at her and snorted. "I may be a lotta different things, Miss Chastity, but believe me, a pimp I'm not. And I'm not talking about you being a prostitute. I'm talking you about you handling yourself like a pro, and doing any and everything with class. I'm talking about stepping up your game, girl. Them guys you fucked at The Meat Club, how much they paid you?"

Chastity blushed. "I never said –"

"How much did they pay you?" Legend repeated.

"A couple of guys gave me two hundred," She said looking down at her lap. "One guy gave me three."

Legend sighed and shook his head. "See, what you don't know is a chick like you – with a little coaching – can get a nigga to slip you four or five hundred just to have you sit with them. And you sure as hell shouldn't be laying up with a nigga who can't break you off a couple'a grand. Shit, girl. You're a fucking gold mine . . . shit, a platinum mine, and you don't even know it."

Chastity sucked her teeth. "Are you crazy? Ain't no nigga gonna give up no C-notes just to have someone sit with them."

Legend grinned. "I'd bet you on it, but like I said, I don't take money from women. But give me a couple of months and see if I don't know what the hell I'm talking about."

Chastity turned and looked out the window. Shit, she thought, if she could pull in money like that she wouldn't have to be dancing at The Meat Club. And she and Jackie could move to a new and better apartment, and maybe she could get her GED and save enough money to put herself through college. Which had been her father's dream for her. "So, you're going to train me, huh?"

"Yeah, I'ma train you."

"Why? So you can fuck me, too?"

Legend dropped her hand. "Yo, ma. Why you gotta come at me like that, huh?"

Chastity gave a little chuckle. "Yeah, that's what I thought."

"Well, maybe that's why you don't get paid for thinking," Legend said roughly. "Naw, shortie. I ain't trying to fuck you."

"Swear?"

"What?"

"Swear right now that this just a professional thing. That you ain't trying to just get in my pants," Chastity said in a teasing voice.

Legend paused, then sighed. "Fuck it. I swear to you we'll keep in on a professional basis, and you don't have to worry about me fucking you or anything. You got my word on that."

"What about Jackie? You gonna train her, too?"

"Jackie?" Legend frowned. "Oh, your girlfriend at the club, huh? Naw, ma. She ain't got what it takes."

"Why not? She's pretty."

79

Shay

"I ain't say she ain't pretty. She's very pretty, but she doesn't have what you have. That star quality. I'm glad you're trying to look out for your girl, but if she ain't got it, fuck it, she ain't got it." Legend paused. "So what's the deal, ma? You two sewn together at the hips or something?"

Chastity shook her head. "No, I'm not saying all that. But Jackie's always looked out for me. I can't just abandon her."

"No one says you have to. Loyalty's a good thing. Roll with it. But don't let it hold you back." Legend picked up Chastity's hand again. "Look, tell you what. From here on out, you and Jackie work for me. But here's the thing. Technically, I'm hiring you as dancers. You'll both get $200 a night, and a guarantee of three nights a week. I'm thinking you'll average about another $400 in tips, so you'll be raking in $600 a night."

Chastity nodded, thinking: *Damn near two thousand a week. That'll work.*

"The sweet thing is you don't have to strip; you get to dance with your clothes on," Legend continued. "Most of the people are my parties are dudes, ballers and shit. Some of them bring their girls, but most don't. Your job is to be around and be sexy as hell, smile, and don't turn anyone down if they want to dance. Got it?"

"Got it." She paused. "And for that we get almost two grand a week?"

Legend grinned. "See, already you're moving up in the world, girl."

"I'm feeling this already. So are we working the upstairs parties or the downstairs parties?"

"Oh, you know about those, do you?" Legend tapped her gently on the chin.

80

"Word gets around, boy." Chastity laughed.

"I only give my special downstairs parties two or three times a month, but for now you're working the upstairs parties only. But while you're working for me, I'm going to be grooming you, okay? When I think you're ready I'll promote you to the downstairs parties. But in the meantime I'ma be teaching you little tricks, and shit."

"Like what?"

"Well . . ." Legend paused. "Let's walk around for a minute, okay?"

Chastity nodded, and almost reached over and opened her car door, but then stopped, remembering Legend's earlier instructions. She smiled. "I'll wait for you to open my door, of course."

"Of course, but here's how you do it?"

Chastity laughed. "There's a trick to that?"

"Girl, there's a trick to everything. Okay, we're parked, and you see me get out the car. As soon as I do, you pick up your bag, and start rifling through it. Give the guy enough time to walk over to your side of the car. As soon as he walks around, you close your bag and look at him through your window and smile. If he wasn't planning on opening your car door, he'll get the hint and do it. And that makes him realize you expect to be treated like a lady without him feeling pressured into feeling he has to. Niggas like shit like that. They like women to just expect them to do the gentlemen thing without demanding it."

He opened his car door. "Okay, let's try this."

Chastity dutifully started looking through her bag, stopping as soon as Legend had reached her side of the car. She smiled up at him, and he opened the car and helped her out. He then offered her his arm, and she

81

tucked her hand into the crook of his elbow. He gently removed it.

"No, when I offer you my arm, you just put your hand gently on top of it. Let the man decide to tuck you're your hand in. He has to feel in control at all times, okay?"

"Okay."

They strolled up and down the block a couple of times, Legend giving her various tips on how to walk, how to smile at the appropriate times, and even how to look at a man when he's talking. "Look at him directly in his eyes, but never in a challenging way. You don't want him to feel uncomfortable, just that you're interested. If he tells a corny joke, don't laugh, but do smile. That's one way niggas can tell if a girl is trying to play him, when he tells a corny joke and she busts out laughing like he's Chris Rock."

He finally walked her back to the car, but before beeping the door open with the remote, he smoothed his hand over her hair. "Chastity, Chastity, Chastity. You're the shit, girl. You really are. I'm glad we met."

He stroked her on the cheek, and her heart started racing. "And I'm going to make sure you're glad we met. You got a friend in me, girl. And don't ever forget it."

She started breathing hard as his gaze intensified, and she readied herself for the kiss she knew they were getting ready to share, eagerly anticipating the softness of his lips and the feel of his arms around her waist. But just as he began to lower his face towards her, he suddenly stopped – a frown appearing on his face as if he suddenly remembered something. He straightened up, took a couple of quick breaths, and said, "So, okay. This is been a pretty good night, huh?" He opened the

car door and she climbed in, wondering what the hell had just happened.

Twenty minutes later they were back at the club. "You want me to tell Jackie y'all are working for me or do you wanna tell her, ma?" he said as they walked inside.

"Let me tell her. Oh look, she's on stage now."

Legend watched in silence as Jackie did her thing, then waited until she walked off stage before turning to Chastity. "She's good, but she's no Chastity Jones."

Chapter Four

"Damn, I shoulda taken you up on it when you wanted me to move in with you last year, Chas. This place is the shit." Jackie clicked the remote to change the station on the large plasma television on the wall in the spacious white-on-white sunken living room. The room was full of white roses, to match the rugs and leather furniture, and the light bouquet filled the room as if someone had sprinkled rose water throughout the house.

"Yeah, well, your place ain't half bad," Chastity said, from the kitchen as she tossed a garden salad.

"Shit, yeah my place is bad, but still I ain't livin' large like this. But then I can't fuckin' afford to pay no damn $4,000 a month in rent."

Chastity giggled. "Maintenance fee, you mean. Richard bought me the apartment, remember? In my name, free and clear; even though he's the one paying the maintenance fee."

Jackie shook her head. "Damn, if you ain't got the hook-up. I was busy pushin' up on that fuckin' quarterback at the Super Bowl after party last year, and you . . . I look over and see you hemmed up in the corner with some little white man with horn-rimmed glasses, and I felt sorry for you. And shit if it wasn't the owner of the fuckin' team."

"Hell yeah," Chastity said as she sat down on the leather couch next to Jackie. "Why fuck with the

84

players with you can hook up with the man who pays their salaries."

"Yeah, I gotta give it to ya, bitch. You the shit. And then you ain't even got to fuck the bastard but maybe three or four times a year. You got the real hook-up."

"Hmph," Chastity said. "Actually, I don't even fuck him. All that motherfucker does is eat my pussy for like an hour and then spend another hour sitting on the chair with nothing but a pair of black socks on, jerking off while he watches me masturbate."

"Another fuckin' freak. Least he ain't as bad as that A-rab from . . ." Jackie wrinkled her nose. "Where's he from, again?"

"Dubai."

"Yeah, from there. That's the one that likes you to stick a 10-inch dildo in his ass while he wears a collar and laps up piss from a dog's bowl."

Chastity nodded. "A diamond-studded collar worth about thirty grand and a solid gold dog bowl that's gotta be worth another five."

"How much does the piss cost?"

The two women started laughing so hard Chastity almost choked on her salad.

"Girl, leave my Arab freak alone. That sand nigger's about to buy me a 2009 Maybach 62."

Jackie slammed her hand down on the white marble coffee table. "Get the fuck outta here, bitch! Are you kiddin' me? Damn, that's what's up! Them muthafuckas cost like five-hundred grand, right? Shit, I know you gonna let me drive that shit. Whatchoo gonna do with your Benz? You tradin' that shit in?"

"Uh uh. Like I said, he's gonna buy the Maybach for me, and you best believe that bitch is

gonna be in my name. So why would I trade my Benz in when that's all paid for, too? Shit, I don't mind pushing two luxury rides. Legend's got four."

"Yeah, but at least he be drivin' his shit. You be taxi cabbin' it most of the time."

Chastity shrugged. "Only in the daytime. I don't like driving in New York City traffic. I don't mind driving at night, though."

"Shit, let someone buy me a Benz or a Maybach. I'd not only be drivin' all day, I'd be sleeping and showering in that mofo."

"Yeah, well, it ain't like you gotta be hoofing it, Jackie. Or like you're paying your own rent."

"Yeah, my Lexus is cool as shit, and like I said, my apartment's bad. I'm not livin' as large you, but between Jerrod and Gerald, I'm doing a whole lot more than okay."

Chastity snorted. "I still can't figure out how you messing with two niggas with almost identical names."

"Yeah, well, I still can't figure out to juggle six or seven niggas like you without fuckin' up somewhere down the line. This way if one of them is fuckin' the shit outta me and I call out the wrong name they don't even realize it."

The girls started laughing again.

"But you know, Chas," Jackie said after a minute. "Look at how we livin', and we ain't even twenty-years-old yet. Who woulda thought two little girls from 132nd Street would be doin' it up like this, man? Ya know? My family ain't never had more than a fuckin' pot to piss in, and your family, well, you know your family."

"Yeah mom a ho and my dad a murderer."

"Hey, girl, I wasn't gonna say your mom was no ho," Jackie said quickly.

"Yeah, well she was. And I know it, you know it, and everyone on 132nd Street knew it. My dad busted his ass, working overtime and shit, to get her everything she wanted, and she still was creeping on him." Chastity grew silent for a moment. "And don't think I didn't love my mom, I really did. And I don't think she deserved to be killed. I do miss her. But I miss my dad more. You know I was always daddy's little girl. And he was the wronged one in this whole shit, and he's the one who's on death row."

Jackie moved closer to Chastity and started rubbing her back. "But ain't you say that lawyer guy is working to get his sentence suspended or somethin'?"

"No, he's appealing the death sentence is all." Chastity took a deep breath. "I don't think my dad's ever going to get out of prison, though. But as long as I can talk to him on the phone and go visit him, that's at least something, ya know?"

"Yeah, girl, I know."

Chastity couldn't help it. Tears filled her eyes as they did every time she thought about her father's situation. She made sure she kept money on his books, and she talked to him every day now, thanks to the cell phone arrangement Legend hooked up, and she had one of New York's most well-known defense lawyer working on his case, but there was still a chance New York State was going to kill her father. It just didn't seem fair. Their new attorney had told her that if the court-appointed attorney had used a plea for temporary insanity during the first trial, her father might have actually gotten off -- especially since he didn't have a criminal record, had a spotless work history, and because

it would be understandable for someone for to experience rage when actually seeing a spouse in the act of betrayal. But the court-appointed lawyer was fresh out of law school, and never raised the defense, and there wouldn't have been money for psychologists or psychiatrists to back up the claim even if he had. Now there was money available – thanks to the significant change in Chastity's circumstances – but appeal judges normally won't overturn a case because the first lawyer didn't choose the correct defense.

"You know what? Let's get out of here," Chastity said, jumping up from the couch and grabbing her pocketbook and keys. "I don't feel like just sitting around and being depressed."

"But I was just gonna watch –" Jackie looked at the opening credits of her favorite soap opera, *All My Children*, then sighed and clicked off the television. "Aight, where we goin'?"

"Let's go shopping. I still want to get that leather raincoat I saw in the Bloomingdale's catalogue," Chastity said, rattling the set of car keys she'd just fished out her pocketbook.

"Yeah, aight, but let's stop around the way, first. I promised my mom a couple of hundred dollars for a party she's throwin' for my brother." Jackie snatched the keys from Chastity's hand. "And I'll drive. I don't mind fuckin' with traffic, and I wanna be riding up the block in style. Show them jealous bitches what we workin' with and shit."

Chastity looked in the vanity mirror on the passenger side of the car as Jackie weaved in and out of traffic. Her makeup was impeccable, her eyebrows perfectly arched, and her hair was fierce. Good. Still, she put on another coat of lip gloss for good measure. She

and Jackie always made it a point to look the very best when they went up to 132nd Street these days. The two of them had generated a lot of gossip when people found out that the were dancing at The Meat Club, and when word got back to the block, whenever they ran into one of the girls they knew from 132nd Street they had to put up with snide remarks and finger pointing. But in the two years since they hooked up with Legend, they still generated a lot of finger pointing from the 132nd Street bitches, but not because they looked down on them, but because they were jealous. They didn't know what she and Jackie were into, but they knew they were into something big, because they were always iced up when they rode up on the block in a luxury car and dressed like they were high-fashion models.

"Ready to do this?" Jackie said as she pulled up in front of their old building.

"Hell yeah," Chastity said as she opened her car door and climbed out.

Just like every summer afternoon, the block was crowded with young girls who thought they looked fly and wanting to show off what they got, and young boys checking them out and trying to figure out which girl to push up on and maybe score a piece of action for that night. But when Chastity and Jackie stepped out the car, all eyes were on them. Chastity was wearing a sky blue silk Ralph Lauren sleeveless blouse with a flowing white linen skirt and four and half inch blue and white Jimmy Choo stiletto heel sandals. Jackie was rocking a mint green Michael Kors shorts set, with green Manolo Blahnik sandals. They both paused once they got out the car – striking a pose -- and made a production of taking off their Gucci sunglasses before strutting inside the building, heads held high and their noses in the air.

Shay

"You see them jealous bitches grittin' on us?" Jackie said with a little chuckle. "Especially Pookie. I hate that stuck up bitch with her thirty dollar weave and her blubber lips."

"Yeah, I saw them. Fuck 'em," Chastity said as she pressed the button to summon the elevator.

"Her brother is foine, though! Did you see him?" Jackie licked her lips as they rode up to the third floor. "Doin' that state bid did John-John some good. You seent them muscles? Made my pussy flutter just looking at them. I wonder if his dick is as big as biceps. Too bad he's just another broke nigga."

"Hey, Miss Joyce," Chastity said when Jackie's mother opened the door. "How are you doing today?"

"Hey, Ma. What's up?"

"How you girls doing?" Miss Joyce stepped aside and let the young women into the apartment. "I'm just in here trying to clean up a little for the party on Saturday. I know y'all coming, right?"

"Yeah, Ma, I'ma be here. I don't know about Chas, though." Jackie said pulling out her wallet. "But here's a little something to help you with the expenses. I know you only said you needed like five hundred, but I'm doing pretty good right about now, so how about I hit you off with seven?"

"Thanks, baby," Miss Joyce gave Jackie a big hug. "Y'all come on in and have a seat. Want some ice tea? I just made a pitcher. And I'm getting ready to fry up some chicken. Can y'all stay for dinner?"

"Naw, ma. We gotta split."

"Right now? Can't y'all even stay a minute? You just got here!"

"I'm going to stop through for the party, too, Miss Joyce," Chastity said. "And if you didn't buy the

90

liquor yet I'll have someone drop you off a case of Johnny Walker Black sometime tomorrow. My own little contribution to the festivities."

"Thank you, honey. That would be real nice. But you sure y'all can't even stay a minute? You girls are always on the run. I hardly see either of you anymore." Miss Joyce turned to Jackie. "I know you busy with that boyfriend of yours . . . what's his name again?"

"Jerry," Jackie said, while Chastity tried to suppress a smile. Jackie was covering her bases by giving the name Jerry. That way whichever one she brought around, Gerald or Jerrod, she could still play it off.

"Yeah, Jerry. I know you're busy with him, but you can still come around. And you can bring him around. I still ain't seen this Mr. Big Shot who you got taking care of you." Miss Joyce looked pissed. "If you want a man to respect you you've got to let him meet your folks. So he knows you come from good stock."

"Ma, Jerry respects me, and I'ma see if I can get him to come with me on Saturday, but no promises, okay?" Jackie kissed her mother on the cheek. "But for real, we gotta get outta here. Chastity has an appointment with her lawyer to talk about her father's case, and we can't be late. You know how these Jewish lawyers are. You five minutes late and they done moved on to the next client."

"Oh! Well, then that's different. How's your daddy doing, Chastity? Tell him we all praying for him."

"Yes, ma'am. I'll let him know."

Jackie waited until they were on the elevator before turning to Chastity and saying: "You ain't even got to say shit. I'm sorry. But it was the only excuse I could come up with that would get us up outta there."

Chastity's jaw tightened. "Yeah? Well, it was still fucked up."

They stepped out in the bright sunlight, and struck poses while putting their sunglasses back on. "Don't turn your head, but look at Pookie, whispering in Fee-Fee's ear," Jackie said in a low voice. "You know them bitches are talkin' 'bout us. I should go over there and fuck 'em up just on principle."

"You always want to kick someone's ass. But I got a better idea," Chastity said. "Pookie's still fucking with Boogie, right? Watch my shit." She turned to face the small group of girls off to the left and waved in their direction, as if just noticing them. Then she leaned back on the building and smiled at a tall skinny light-skinned dude who was standing a little off to the side. Once she knew she had his attention, she crooked her finger at him, beckoning him over. He paused and looked in Pookie's direction, but only for a second before scurrying over.

"Hey, Chastity. You lookin' good, ma. What you been up to, girl?" he said, trying to come off cool, but unable to hide his excitement and nervousness as he shifted from one foot to another.

"I'm just chilling, Boogie. Me and Jackie had to stop off to see her moms," Chastity said in flirtatious voice. "Plus, you know, we wanted to see some of our old friends. Like you, dude. What have you been into lately?"

"Nothing much, but I know what I want to get into," Boogie said, licking his lips and looking her up and down.

"Oh, and what's that?" Chastity said with a forced giggle.

"Girl, I think you know what I'm talkin' 'bout," Boogie said, stepping closer, obviously more confident.

"Hmm . . . I know what I wish you were talking about; but aren't you supposed to going with Pookie?" Chastity said with a little pout.

"Naw, man. She and I kick it from time-to-time, but ain't nothing serious. I'm a free man, looking for a free woman."

"Is that right?" Chastity put the tip of her sunglasses in mouth and gave it a little lick. "Well, one thing I've learned is nothing worth having is free, but I'm certainly open to talk about possibilities."

"Boogie, can I speak to you a minute?" Pookie's shrill voice rang out. Chastity didn't bother to turn her head to look at her, but from the corner of her eye she could see the girl was fuming. She had one hand on her skinny hip and the other balled up in a fist by her side.

"Is that your master's voice calling?" Jackie said, speaking for the first time.

"Man, I ain't got no master," Boogie shot back, although he took a quick look in Pookie's direction, then tried to wave her off.

"Boogie, I'm not playing," Pookie said even louder. The girls around her were wide-eyed but silent, as if waiting to see what was going to jump off. "Come here *now!*"

"Boogie, why don't you go see what she wants, but hurry up back 'cause I want to finish talking to you," Chastity said, moving in close to him. "Cause you know, I'm not busy tonight, so I bet we can find a lot to talk about."

"Aight, aight, but I'ma be right back," Boogie said eagerly. "Don't go nowhere."

Shay

Jackie waited until he walked off before saying, "Girl, you ain't shit! Oh, man, Pookie is tight! You really fucked her good, and right in front of all her friends. Look at her lettin' him have it. I betcha she's gonna slap the shit outta him. I know she know betta than to think she's gonna slap the shit outta you."

Chastity snorted. "Nah, she's not gonna try that shit. She hasn't forgot how I use to wax that ass when we were back in elementary school. And anyway, we ain't finished with her stank ass yet," Chastity said, elbowing Jackie. "There's goes John-John coming up the block again. Work your shit, girl."

"Hey, John-John," Jackie called out to the short muscle-bound man walking toward Pookie and Boogie. "Come here a minute."

Pookie was so engrossed with Boogie, pointing her finger in his face and damn near frothing at the mouth that she didn't even notice her younger brother approaching Jackie.

"What's up, girl?" he said when he reached them. "I ain't seen you in a minute."

"You're what's up," Jackie replied, running her hands over his bulging biceps. "Lookin' all fine and shit. When you get out, man?"

"Last week. And you lookin' pretty fine your damn self, ma."

"Really?" Jackie did a little twirl in front of John-John. "'Bout time you noticed, boy. I been feelin' you for awhile, but you ain't never seem to have no time for your home girl."

"Shit, girl, you ain't never acted like you wanted to give a young nigga the time of day," John-John said with a suspicious look on his face.

94

"Well, damn, I been waitin' on you to say something to me. But I been wantin' to spend some time with you," Jackie said. "Haven't I, Chas?"

"Hell yeah," Chastity said on cue. "She's been up in my ear for a minute now, talking about you."

"Word?" John-John smiled. "Well, here I am."

"And here I am," Jackie said, putting her arms around his neck. "So whatchoo wanna do, boy?"

"John-John, get your young ass ova here!" Pookie yelled out suddenly, causing some of the girls around her to start laughing and John-John to blush.

"Damn," Chastity said, while scanning the area for Boogie. "What? She got you on a leash or something?" She spotted Boogie a little off to the side of Pookie and gave him a one arm shrug as if to say "What's up?" and he hurriedly put one finger up in a "just a minute" signal.

"Hold up, Pookie," John-John told his sister. "I'm talkin'."

"Yeah? Well, I *said*, come here."

"And *I* said, hold the fuck up," John-John said in a loud voice. "What the fuck is wrong with you?"

"Bring your stupid ass here and I'll tell you what's wrong with me," Pookie shot back.

"Damn, and I thought you was old enough to handle your business," Jackie said as if she were really disappointed. "You go ahead 'fore she pops a vein. Maybe when, you know, you're old enough to do you we can hook up."

"Shit, I'm old enough to do me now. And I sure as hell wanna do you, ma."

"Yeah? Well then I suggest you man up and let her know, cause I'm lookin' for somethin' to get into

tonight. And I was sure as hell was lookin' forward to you gettin' into you."

"I'm right with you, ma. Let me handle this real quick." He gave Jackie a quick squeeze on the waist, then turned and stomped off towards his sister. "Man, what the fuck is wrong with you?" he asked her.

"The fuck wrong with me?" Pookie snapped at him. "Nigga, you done lost your mind?"

Chastity noticed Boogied walk off from the crowd, motioning her to follow. But instead she said, "Come on, Jackie." The two women walked over and leaned against her car, then Chastity shot Boogie a look that said, "What's up?"

He glanced at Pookie, who was still yelling at John-John, then furtively walked over to Chastity.

"So what you 'bout to do?" he said in a low voice.

'I was waiting on you to tell me. I didn't mean to cause no trouble between you and Pookie, but you said –"

"Yeah, I'm tellin' you ain't no real shit with us. She just felt like mouthing off," he said quickly.

"Well, if you say so," Chastity said, giving him a knowing look.

"Don't worry. I put that bitch in her place. She ain't gonna say shit else."

"So good, we gonna kick it tonight, then, right?" Chastity licked her lips.

"Yeah, girl, we kickin' it. Where you wanna go?"

"You got your own place, right? Ain't no sense in paying for a hotel. Give me some money so I can get us some Moet and I'll meet you upstairs in like fifteen minutes."

96

"Moet?" Boogie started looking nervous.

"Yeah, that's all I drink. Too rich for your blood?" Chastity said in a teasing voice, trailing her fingers over his cheek.

"Naw, ma. I got you." He looked over to see if Pookie was looking, then reached into his pocket and then put a couple of crumbled bills in Chastity's hand. "This should do it. Hurry up back."

"You want to ride with us to the store?" Chastity said, knowing he wouldn't dare get in the car while Pookie was still out there. He might have been fronting, but he wasn't trying to front that hard.

"Naw, I'ma handle some business, but I'll meet you upstairs in like fifteen."

Chastity waited until she saw Pookie look over in their direction, then made a big deal of holding the money Boogie had given her, and smoothing out the wrinkles. "Okay, thanks, Boogie," she said before slowly sticking the money in her bra.

"Oh no, the fuck you didn't!" they both turned at the sound of Pookie's voice and saw her rushing at them.

Jackie hit the remote control and said, "Chas, get in the car."

Chastity waved her hand dismissively and said, "I got this."

"Naw, for real, get in the car, cause I gotta handle something real quick," Jackie said urgently.

Chastity shrugged, and got in the passenger seat, then watched as Jackie walked off and Pookie and Boogie started arguing violently. *She better not try and do something to me or my ride, or I swear I'll get out and tap dance on her ass.*

She looked over, trying to spot Jackie, and saw her talking to John-John. Two minutes later he pulled

97

her into a grinding hug, then Jackie walked back to the car, brushing past Pookie and Boogie.

"Excuse me, you two," Jackie said as she reached for the driver's car door. "And Pookie, tell your fine-ass brother I said thanks for the C-note." She got in the car, stuck the key in the ignition and pushed the button to roll down the window. "Ta-ta," she said, twirling her fingers. She pulled off just as Pookie bitch-slapped Boogie, and was pimp-slapped in return. Chastity turned in her seat as the car drove up the block and saw John-John rush over and punch Boogie in the head, and in the next second the two were brawling on the sidewalk like two prize-fighters.

"Mmmm . . . 132nd Street gonna be live tonight," Chastity said as she saw one of Boogie's friends jump in the fight, and then a friend of John-John's do the same.

"That'll teach that bitch to be fuckin' with us," Jackie said, laughing so hard she almost hit a parked car. "We done fucked her with both her man and her brother."

"Damn, you don't feel sorry for her?" Chastity as she watched Pookie dancing around her brother and her man as if trying to figure out whose side to jump on.

"Hell, naw," Jackie answered.

"Not even a little bit?"

"Not in the fuckin' least."

"Good," Chastity said, fastening her seat belt. "Cause neither do I. Now, let's go shopping."

Chapter Five

"Hey, what are you doing around this way?" Legend asked as he opened the door to the brownstone he called home. "I didn't think I'd see you until next week."

"I know, but I need a favor," Chastity said, walking in and taking a seat on the black leather couch. "Jackie's mom is giving a party this weekend and yesterday I said I'd send her over a case of Johnny Walker Black. Now I'm going to have to send her over two because I said I'm going to the party but I'm going to hit the tables at A.C. instead with Jamal. It's his birthday. You got me covered?"

"No problem, I got you. So why that cheap nigga taking you to Atlantic City instead of Vegas?" Legend asked as he walked over to the refrigerator behind the bar and pulled out two bottles of Evian. He twisted off the caps and gave one to Chastity.

Chastity shrugged. "Don't know and don't care." She took off her stiletto heels and rubbed her feet before leaning back and letting her toes grip into the plush black carpet.

"I hear ya," Legend sat down on the love seat across from her. "So, what you been up to? You going to the Essence Festival in New Orleans next month?"

"Yeah, I missed it last year 'cause Raheem wanted to take me to Aruba. But I'll be there this year." She took grateful sip of the bottled water. "You going?"

Shay

"Yeah, I thinking about making it. Maybe you can be my date for the Rick Ross concert. He's supposed to be headlining that Saturday night. Or are you flying out there with someone?"

Chastity shook her head. "Nope. I'll be on my own." She knew better than to get her hopes up when Legend said things like "be my date," because the outings were always the same. Wonderful, unforgettable, and even romantic, but they all ended with Legend dropping her off with a quick kiss on the cheek before getting back in his car and driving home, leaving her to take long hot baths with only her butterfly vibrator for company.

"Good. I'll book us a couple of suites at the Ritz Carlton," Legend was saying.

"They're probably already full, Legend."

"Shit, don't you remember who you fucking with? A nigga got connects," Legend said with a smile.

"You the man," Chastity said, holding her bottle of water up for a toast.

"And you the woman," Legend said, touching his bottle to hers.

"Yeah, but I'm the nigga," another male voice, with the same baritone as Legend's but a helluva lot more attitude. Chastity looked up to see a man about the same age and height as Legend, 6-4, but built like a linebacker. His hair was short, but not too short to hide a head full of loose curls; not the kind that looked processed and greasy, but the soft natural curls that were made for a woman to run her fingers through. Curls that were jet black, and just a shade darker than the man's deep chocolate complexion. The man was fine, and Chastity was instantly intrigued. She sat up as he crossed the room and exchanged a quick dab with Legend.

100

"Yo, cuz, what's up, man?" Legend said. "And how'd you get in? I didn't hear the doorbell."

"Rina was coming in with a bag of groceries," the man said, referring to the woman hired to come clean the house every other day, "I came in with her." He turned his attention to Chastity, who had crossed her legs and was smiling engagingly. "And who's this beautiful young lady?" He cocked his head to the side and looked at her little more closely, then grinned. "Never mind, cuz. This has got to be Chastity."

"Chastity Jones, this is my cousin, Hunter Foster," Legend said with, a strange look on his face, which Chastity ignored.

"Cousin?" Chastity said as Hunter walked over and kissed her hand. The softness of his lips reminded her of Legend's. And now that he was up close she saw that his smooth complexion had red undertones, like Legend's; though he was much darker.

"You look even more beautiful in real life than you do in your picture," he said graciously, looking upward at her from his still crouched position. "I've been dying to meet you."

"You've seen pictures of me?" Chastity asked in surprise.

"Just the one Legend has in his bedroom, but it doesn't do you justice."

Chastity looked over at Legend, who was sitting gripping his bottle of water with a tightened jaw. *Legend has a picture of me in his bedroom? I've never seen it.*

"Someone snapped a photo of us at the NBA All-Star game a couple of months ago," Legend said quickly, as if reading her thoughts. "I thought I'd shown it to you. I'll get you a copy if you'd like." He turned to his cousin. "What brings you up this way?"

"Business, but it can wait," Hunter said, taking a seat on the couch next to Chastity and letting his leg brush up against her, sending a thrill through her body. "I've been trying to get Legend to introduce us for more than a year now, girl. But now that I've seen you up close, I can see why he's been keeping you under wraps." He looked over at Legend. "Scared of a little competition, huh, cuz?"

"Hmph." Legend's lips curled into a sneer. "Like you'd be competition."

"Well, how about we let Miss Chastity here decide that?" Hunter said, patting her on the hand, giving her a view of a diamond crusted ring with a platinum initial "H" in the middle.

"I've heard of sibling rivalry, but I didn't know it extended to cousins." Chastity leaned back on the couch. "And I'm certainly not going to get into the middle of it."

"Well, normally we don't compete over women, but damn, girl, you're a superwoman," Hunter said smoothly. "And you know what they say, every superwoman needs a superman." He grinned, and added in a sing song voice. "*Here I am.*"

"I fuckin' hate that song," Legend grumbled, shaking the now empty Evian bottle.

"Man, that Rick Ross shit is the jam," Hunter said.

"Yeah, well, Rick Ross ain't shit," Legend shot back, causing Chastity to look at him in surprise. Didn't he just ask her to be his date at the Rick Ross concert at Essence? *Okay, this shit is getting deep. Let me get the hell outta here before it gets heavy, too.* She looked at her watch. "Well, it's getting late and I do need to be getting out of here."

"Already?" Hunter said, disappointment evident in his voice.

"Yeah," Chastity said, trying to hide her reluctance as she stood up. "I just needed to speak to Legend about something real quick. It was nice meeting you, though."

"Well, are you driving? Or can I give you a lift?" Hunter asked.

"Don't worry about me, I can catch a cab," Chastity said. "Besides, didn't you say you and Legend had some business to talk about?"

"Yeah, but I also said it could wait." Hunter stood up.

Chastity looked over at Legend to gauge his reaction, but his face was expressionless. "Well, I –"

"My ride's right outside," Hunter said, offering her his arm. She hesitated, and glanced at Legend again, but he simply shrugged. She then put her hand lightly on Hunter's arm, and he immediately tucked it into his elbow.

"I can't believe we've never met before," Chastity said, once they were inside his red 2009 Porsche 911 Turbo convertible and weaving in and out of the traffic on Fifth Avenue. "Legend's never even mentioned you."

Hunter pulled a pair of sunglasses from a clip on the driver's side visor, and put them on, almost hitting a taxi while doing so – and not seeming to care. "That's not surprising. Legend is like me, we don't talk a lot about our private lives. We like it to keep it . . . well, we like to keep it private. Although," Hunter turned to look at her as he stopped for a red light, "I would think he might have let you in on a few things."

"Why's that?" Chastity said, glad that he had put on the glasses; she found his eyes almost as distracting as she had found his cousin's that first night that they met at The Meat Club.

Hunter shrugged. "I just thought he might open up to you."

"Well, he's told me a little about himself, but not much. I know he was born in Los Angeles, Watts, and that he came to New York when he was nineteen."

Hunter nodded. "That's right. Has he ever talked about his family, though?"

"No, not really. And as you said, he's a very private person, so I never tried to pry."

"Well, my parents were killed when I was ten –"

"Oh," Chastity's hand flew to her mouth, "I'm so sorry."

"It was a long time ago," Hunter said sullenly. "There was a shootout between the Crips and the Bloods, and my father got caught in the crossfire. He was square, ain't had nothing to do with shit, just happened to be crossing the street at the wrong time. My mother always had a weak heart, and she had a heart attack when she found out what happened. We had a double funeral a few days later."

"Oh, God," Chastity said softly.

"I moved in with Legend and his family, and his parents treated me like I was theirs, so he and I grew up like brothers," Hunter continued. "I came up to Harlem in 2001 on some business, and liked it so much I stayed. I was the one who convinced Legend to come out here. He liked it, too." Hunter threw back his head and laughed. "Shit, what's not to like? Best move either one of us coulda made."

Chastity watched Hunter as he continued maneuvering through the midtown traffic. The physical similarities between him and Legend were few, besides their shared height and their mesmerizing eyes, but they both had an easy comfortable manner about them, a confidence that was intoxicating and contagious. But while Legend had a touch of mystery about him, Hunter had an underlying touch of sadness, which she found endearing. It made him seem almost vulnerable, though nothing about him suggested weakness. In fact, Hunter had thug written all over him. Not so much in the way he dressed, but in his swagger and his attitude.

"Are you and Legend still as close as you were when you were kids?" she asked, still wondering why she'd never met him.

"Well, yes and no," Hunter said slowly. "He and I run in different circles, and neither of us are big on socializing unless it has to do with business, so we don't see each other too often, but yeah . . . we're still close. Ain't nothing I wouldn't do for that nigga, and I know he feels the same way about me." He looked at Chastity. "And I know he really cares about you, too. He told me you were kinda like the little sister neither one of ever had."

"He said that?"

"Yeah." Hunter chuckled. "You ain't see how bent outta shape he was when I was flirting with you? He probably thought it was like incest or some shit." He threw back his head. "Shit, he might feel like a brother for you, but my feelings are entirely different."

"Boy, stop playing," Chastity said, playfully hitting him on his arm. "You just met me. Don't be handing me no corny line about you having any kind of feelings for me."

Shay

"Oh, so I'm corny now, huh?" Hunter grinned. "Okay, let me put it like this. I got feelings toward you, okay?" He suddenly turned serious. "And I think I could have feelings for you, given some time. And I intend to spend the time, if you're game."

"How do you think Legend would feel about that?" Chastity said in a teasing voice.

"Shit, let that nigga find his own woman," Hunter said, putting his arm around her shoulders and pulling her closer to him. "I think I just found mine."

"I'm telling you, Jackie, the nigga is all that," Chastity said. "Look at all this shit he bought me."

"I'm lookin', I'm lookin'," Jackie said, going through the array off dresses spread on Chastity's bed and picking up a blue Armani mini and holding it up against her own body. "This shit is the truth."

"Oh yeah," Chastity said, "and after he dropped like $20,000 on me at Lord & Taylor's he took me to Winston's –"

"Winston's? The jewelry store?" Jackie's mouth dropped open.

"The jewelry boutique," Chastity corrected her. "And look at this, shit." She pulled an array of boxes from a small shopping bag sitting by the bed. "He got me jewelry for every fucking outfit we bought. Blue sapphires earrings and necklace for that dress –"

"Fuck!" Jackie dropped the blue Armani dress and grabbed the jewelry box out of Chastity's hand. She gasped as she looked at the pear-shaped sapphire

106

earrings and pendant trimmed in diamonds. "How much did this shit cost?"

Chastity plopped down on the bed, grinning. "You wouldn't believe me if I told you."

"Try me, bitch."

"Well, $12,000 for the –"

"Damn, girl! He spent $12,000 for this set? Sweet!" Jackie said holding the earrings up to the light.

"Naw, girl. $12,000 for the earrings, the pendant cost another twenty-five grand." Chastity crossed her arms under her head. "Then there's the emerald earrings for the green Halston there, and the ruby necklace for the red Versace --"

"Stop!" Jackie held her hand up. "I can't take no more."

"Jackie, I'm telling you the nigga dropped a cool one-hundred grand on me this afternoon like it was nothing," Chastity gushed.

"The nigga must be a millionaire," Jackie said breathlessly. "Just what I always wanted . . . a nigganaire."

"Yeah, and he didn't even try and fuck me."

Jackie sucked her teeth. "Stop lyin, bitch. First you tell me you ain't never fucked Legend as much as he puts you down for shit, and now you tellin' me his cuz just spent a hunnert grand on you and he ain't try either? Get the fuck."

"Jackie, you know I've never lied to you. I'm telling you the motherfucker never made a move on me." Chastity smiled and closed her eyes. "But I know he wants to. He probably just wants to check with Legend one more time to make sure he's not stepping on his toes."

Shay

"Or steppin' on his dick," Jackie said as she continued to finger the sapphire earrings.

"Whatever." Chastity grimaced, remembering what Hunter told her about Legend thinking of her like a little sister. Now it made sense, the way he never made a play for her, yet always having her back. Maybe if she played it differently that night after the restaurant, not told him that they had to keep their relationship on a professional level; maybe things would have been different. Tears sprang to her eyes as thought of the opportunity lost just because she was trying to play it cute.

"But, damn, Chas, a hunnert grand is a lot of money for a nigga to put out just to grease the works for him to lay down some pipe later."

"Yeah, I know. But believe me, he got it like that. Never even batted an eye."

"How old is he?" Jackie asked.

"Twenty-six. Just a year older than Legend."

"So, what . . . I guess he's dealing?"

Chastity nodded. "Big time. And only in weight. He told me the whole deal, said he wanted to lay his cards on the table so I know what I'm about to get into."

"How big time is big time?" Jackie asked, finally sitting down on the bed next to Chastity.

"Big fucking time. He actually supplies the dealers. From things he said I'm betting he pulls in at least a two or three hundred grand a month; a couple of million a year. And he's been down for four or five years now, so you know he's rolling in it."

Jackie shivered. "A nigganaire. Youse one lucky ho." She let out a deep breath. "Man, Chas, if you weren't my girl I'd be jealous like a muthafucka."

Chastity shrugged. "Yeah, but that's if I go for it."

"Shit, bitch, as much as this nigga just laid out you know if gets the green light from Legend he's going to expect to be fuckin' you raw on the regular."

"You know, Jackie, one of the first things Legend taught me is to never feel you owe a nigga for what he gives you because you've already earned it. But you know what? I'm really feeling this nigga."

"Yeah, I know."

Chastity lifted her head up from the bed and looked at her friend. "How do you know?" she asked suspiciously.

"Because, I know you," Jackie said simply. "If you ain't fuck Legend it ain't because you ain't want to. And since he's Legend's cousin, he's the next best thing."

"Fuck you, bitch."

"Uh huh," Jackie said. "Pass me the remote. *America's Next Top Model* is about to come on."

Chapter Six

"**Y**ou talk to Legend lately?"

"Mm hm . . . I spoke to him this morning. I had to give him an address for a liquor delivery I needed made for a party tonight," Chastity said as she snuggled closer into Hunter's arms as they did slow danced to a cut from Alicia Keye's latest CD. "Why?"

"He say anything about me?"

"Uh uh. But we didn't really have a chance to talk," Chastity said dreamily. "I caught him at a bad time. He said he was doing inventory or something."

"Damn, girl, you feel good," Hunter said as he ran his fingers down her back. "I'm glad you wore a back out dress so I could feel just how smooth you are. Smooth as silk, baby, smooth as silk."

Chastity undid two of his shirt buttons and slid her hand over his bare chest, glad he wasn't wearing a t-shirt. "Mmm, you don't feel too bad yourself," Chastity said. Hairless, just like Legend, she thought. Smooth and hard. And as she grinded her pelvic into his groin she was glad to know that his chest wasn't the only thing hard.

"Goddamn." Hunter let out a sharp breath. "You gonna make me forget we out in public. I'ma about to throw you down on one of these tables and make you my woman for real."

Chastity grinned up at him, "Really? That would be exciting." She gave one of his nipples a little squeeze.

Hunter moaned. "Baby, baby, baby. Oh, God, what I want to do with you."

"Tell me what you want to do with me." Chastity snuggled her face into the opening in his shirt and gave his chest an enticing lick.

Hunter shivered, then pulled away; holding her at arms length, and looking deeply into her eyes. "If I tell you, I'm going tell you some place where then I can show you."

Chastity unflinchingly met his gaze. "So why are we still here in this club?"

Hunter hesitated, then said, "Don't play with me, Chas. You really want to be with me tonight?"

"I'm not playing with you, and I'm not trying to play you," Chastity said, remembering how she blew it with Legend because she played the coy role. "I know I've known you only two days, but I know what I want, and I want you."

"What if," Hunter finally broke his eyes from hers. "What if it wasn't the way you want it?"

Damn, don't tell me the nigga can't fuck. Shit. Don't tell me he got one of them three-inch dicks. She tried to move in close again, so she could judge his size, but he moved away. *Oh well, maybe he's good at eating pussy.* "Trust me, I know I'm not going to be disappointed," she said in a husky voice.

"Chas, I . . ." he hesitated again.

"What?" Chastity said, trying to keep the frustration out of her voice.

He took a deep breath, then grabbed her hand. "Come on, let's get out of here."

Twenty minutes later they pulled up in front of a small mansion in Long Island. "Follow me," Hunter said gruffly after he unlocked the door and disarmed the

security system. He led her upstairs before she could take a good look around. He opened up the door to what she figured was a bedroom, then pressed her against a wall without even bothering to turn on the lights, kissing her deeply, then moving his mouth down her neck and then down to her cleavage. "Girl, I've been wanting to do this since I first saw you sitting on that couch yesterday." He slipped down the shoulder straps of her dress, baring her breasts. He cupped one in his hands and gave it a squeeze, then licked her nipple, causing her to shiver.

"Mmm," she said, "I like." She put her arms over his shoulders and pushed her body into his. Aw yeah, the nigga's working with at least eight inches, and he's hard as a rock, she thought with satisfaction as they started grinding into each other. *This is going to be a good night after all.* But when she reached down to give his dick a squeeze, he pushed her hand away. She tried again, this time succeeding. She gasped, but with surprise which she hoped he mistook for passion. Yeah, his dick was hard, but a tad too hard. As hard as the plastic dick one of her Japanese men kept in his pants to hide the fact that he only had a couple inches of real dick to offer.

But before she could dwell on her disappointment, Hunter grabbed her by the waist and turned her away from the wall, propelling her backwards until the back of her knees hit the back of a bed, and she fell down into its softness.

She reached up to pull him down on top of her, but he was already on his knees in front of her, moving his hands under her dress and pulling at her thong.

"You smell so sweet," he said as he started nibbling the inside of her thighs.

112

RAW

She moaned, as he slid her dress up over her stomach and started playing with her pubic hair, then started quivering as he began to lick her lips of her pussy. She knew how to fake it, she'd done it with so many men, but the sensations he stirred inside of her were real. He was making her feel like she always knew Legend could . . .she pushed the thought out of her head, and concentrated on the man who was driving her crazy in reality instead of in her fantasies. The man who was using his fingers to open the lips of her pussy, and giving her clitoris a little lick; not a timid lick, but a teasing one. She was experienced enough to know this was a man with experience. But she nearly lost it when he then scraped his teeth over her the tip of her clitoris than gave it a soft nibble, causing every nerve in her body to jump.

"Oh my God," she said, her breath coming in short gasps, "Stop, Hunter, you're going to make me cum."

But he didn't stop, and he didn't answer, instead he inserted the very tip of his now curved tongue, not into her vagina, but in the tiny slit of her urinary opening, causing a sensation she'd never felt before, and never wanted to end. "Oh no, oh no . . . I can't take it," she said, her body doing an involuntary dance on the bed, as she was overcome with an ecstasy. "Please, stop. Oh, please, Hunter, oh fuck," she moaned.

He started alternating between tonguing and nibbling at her clitoris, then put a finger at the slit of her vagina, slowly and deliberately tickling it before pushing it inside. When it was fully in, he started moving it and out, as he slid his body upwards over her, stopping to kiss and nibble her breasts again before making his way up her chest, her throat before kissing her on the lips. "How do you feel?" he said in a husky voice.

113

Shay

"Oh, God, Hunter," was all she could say, unable to fully catch her breath as she continued to twist and writhe.

"Good, that's how I want you to feel," he said in the darkness. He then pushed his finger all of the way inside her, and crooked it.

"Oh shit, right there! You got it right there." Chastity's body bucked wildly. "You got the spot, baby, you got the spot. I'm going to cum, baby!"

But then, to her surprise and disappointment, Hunter pulled his finger out of her pussy, though he continued to play with her clitoris. "Chastity, I wanna cum with you, baby, okay? I wanna feel us cum together."

"Then fuck this pussy," Chastity said without hesitation. At that moment she didn't care if he was only three inches. She wanted him, and she wanted him bad.

"You sure, Chas? You sure you want to do this?" he said as he finally started unzipping his pants.

"Oh goddamn, daddy, I'm sure."

"And you won't have any regrets afterward? No matter what?" he said, sliding his pants down.

"No regrets, Hunter, I swear. I want you so bad, you just don't know," she said, her body dancing up and down on the bed in anticipation.

"Okay, baby, because I really care for you. I really do," he said in a throaty voice, as he played with her clitoris and let his finger dart in and out of her pussy. "You ready for me now?"

"Oh, daddy, I'm so ready," she moaned, opening her legs wide so she could wrap them around his hips as he rode her, which she knew was the best way to keep a small dick in contact with her clitoris and ensure she could reach a climax.

But her eyes flew open as he placed something hard against her opening. That wasn't a three-inch dick she felt trying to push inside her pussy. Was he fucking her with his plastic dildo? But no, it was warm, hard, throbbing flesh, stretching her insides. She was so surprised she stopped moving, and let out a gasp.

Hunter's head jerked back, and he partially pulled out, as he gripped her shoulders tightly. "You okay? Am I hurting you? Do you want me to stop?" he asked, his voice dripping with real concern.

"Stop? Oh, hell no!" She wrapped her legs around his hips and lifted her pelvic up, forcing more of his dick inside of her. "Daddy, I want you to fuck me to death. Now give me that dick."

And he did.

And they came.

And they fucked some more.

And they came over and over again.

"Damn," Hunter said an hour later as he lay on the bed trying to catch his breath. "What are you trying to do? Kill me?"

"Hunter, I know you know a lot about me, so what I'm going to say may sound like a lie, but I've never had a man make love to me like you just did," Chastity said as she trailed her finger down his chest. "Where've you been all my life?"

"Looking for you," he said, grabbing her hand and kissing it hard. "And you didn't know it, but you were looking for me, too."

"Is that right?" Chastity said snuggling into the crook of his arm.

"That's right."

Chastity grinned. "And you had me worried me that you were only working with a pencil dick or something."

"What?" Hunter propped himself on his elbow and looked at her. "I'll have you know I've got nine inches of manhood, lady."

"Felt like ten," Chastity teased.

"Shit, hard as you made me I probably grew another inch." They both started laughing.

"But for real, though, why were you talking about regrets?" Chastity said, when they finally calmed down. "Good as this shit is, how could I ever regret making love to you?"

Hunter reached over and turned on a lamp on the nightstand, flooding the room with light for the first time. "Chas, I got something to tell you."

The serious look on his face gave her a start, and she scrambled into a sitting position, facing him. "What is it?" she said gently.

Hunter looked as if her were going to answer, but then he bit his lip and crossed his hands behind his head, staring up at the ceiling and saying nothing.

"Hunter, what is it?" Chastity prodded. "What happened?"

"Man . . ." he shook his head. "I done fucked up, Chas."

Her stomach felt as if someone dropped a piece of lead at the bottom. "What? Are you married, already?" She lowered her eyes. *Damn, I finally found the perfect man and he's already taken. And I'm so stupid I never even asked.*

"Hell, naw, I ain't married."

Chastity blinked in surprise. "Then what . . . I don't understand."

Hunter took a deep breath. "Chastity, remember when I asked you if you talked to Legend, and if he asked about me?"

She nodded.

"Well, I talked to him yesterday after I took you shopping. And then again this evening, before I picked you up." Hunter turned and looked at her. "And both times he asked me to please not fuck with you."

"He said what? Why? I don't understand." Chastity moved closer to Hunter, as if she thought she might have misheard, or misunderstood his words. "Why would he say something like that? What, he was jealous? You said he only likes me like a sister."

"Yeah, he does. But that's the problem."

"What do you mean?"

"Well," Hunter said slowly. "He knows how I run through women, and he's sure that I'll hurt you. I told him I wouldn't, but he didn't believe me." Hunter shrugged and let out a loud sigh. "Hell, I don't blame him. I've fucked over a buncha women in my life." Hunter sat up in the bed, and took Chastity's hands into his. "But see, I can already tell you're different. I don't know how, you just are. And I swear, Chas, I swear, I'll never fuck you over. Maybe we'll make it, or maybe we won't but I sure as hell wanna try, ma."

Chastity leaned into him, placing a little peck on the lips. "Hunter, baby, I think you should know something more about me. I –"

Hunter grabbed her by the shoulders and pulled her into a long deep kiss. When he finally released her, she was glad she was sitting down, because she felt too weak to stand up. "Chastity, I'm not stupid, okay? I see the way you dress, I see the jewelry you wear, and I saw that big fancy building I dropped you off at on Fifth

Avenue. And I ain't once hear you say something about you having to get up early for work." He chucked her under the chin. "Am I on the right track, ma?"

Chastity took a deep breath, then said, "Uh huh."

"Well, someone's taking care of you, and they're doing it in style. But see, this pussy is mine now," he said grabbing her between the legs. "Drop the nigga. You got yourself a real man now. I can match the motherfucker dollar for dollar."

"Yeah, well," Chastity cleared her throat. "See, it's not a motherfucker. It's motherfuckers."

"Huh?"

"Well, you're right I don't have a job, but there's not just one man taking care of me. There are . . ." she cleared her throat again, "well, there are a few."

Hunter looked at her for a moment, and then said, "Go 'head. I'm listening."

She started from the beginning, starting from her first night at The Meat Club, to her meeting Legend and her working his parties for a year, and then to her series of wealthy 'gentlemen friends,' as she called them. He listened intently, not interrupting her, only nodding his head every now and then to encourage her to continue.

"So, that's my story." She gave a weak smile. "I'm kinda willing to bet your track record with women isn't really too different from mine with men. Use them while they're around, move on to the next when they're not." She looked down at the bed. "I'm surprised Legend didn't tell you."

"Nope. He never said a word about it."

"So," Chastity said slowly, "Where do we go from here?"

"Well, I'd still like to make a go of it. See what happens," Hunter said, rubbing her back as he spoke.

118

"But while we're trying, you gots to be mine, and mine alone. And I mean that shit."

"I think I can do that," Chastity said with a smile.

"I mean that, Chas. 'Cause if you ever fuck me over, I'm going to seriously hurt you. And I'm letting you know that shit up front."

"Don't worry, Hunt, because if you ever try to fuck me over, I'm going to seriously kill you. And I'm letting you know that shit up front."

Hunter grinned. "Well, then let's do this shit, ma."

"Okay," Chastity smiled back at him, as she slid the sheet off his body, and move her lips down to his groin area. "But let's do this shit, first."

Chapter Seven

*H*aving a good time? Chastity looked at the text and frowned. It was from Legend. She and Hunter had decided to hide their relationship from Legend, at least for the time being. At least until it had been going on long enough for him – and them – to see if it was for real. And they'd been careful not to be seen together, for fear of running into him, or someone who might go back and say something to him. In fact, Chastity hadn't even left Hunter's apartment since arriving there Friday night. So why the cryptic message? Had he somehow found out? And how should she answer?

She slapped herself on the forehead. Of course, he thinks I'm in A.C. with Jamal. She quickly typed in a carefully worded text in return: *Having the time of my life. Never felt better, and not sure I ever could. I probably won't be returning to NYC until Tuesday. Check you out then.*

It wasn't really a lie, she thought as she hit the send button. Technically, since Hunter lived in Long Island, she really wasn't in New York City itself. Still, she felt a little guilty texting him bullshit while lying naked in his cousin's bed. She'd never deceived Legend before. She sat there in on the edge of the bed, trying to figure out how exactly she was going to face Legend on Tuesday, just two days away, without out-and-out lying,

when Hunter came out of the shower, drying himself off with a towel while singing *Come Close* by Common.

"What's a gangsta like you doing singing love songs?" Chastity asked, as she walked over and placed her arms around her neck.

"Yeah, how about this, ma?" Hunter grinned. *"We got grams in this bitch, girl, come and get you some."*

Chastity laughed and threw up one hand in the air, and started grinding her pussy against Hunter's still damp body. *"Money makes me cum. Money, money, makes me cum."*

Hunter chuckled. "Ain't you the shit? I bet that's your theme song."

"Yeah, well, I ain't never had any shame about my game," Chastity said, kissing him. "But for real, I'd want you even if you were a broke nigga."

"Word?"

"Word."

"Yeah, well, let's hope we neva hafta test that shit. Besides, like they say – it ain't trickin' if you got it." Hunter gently moved Chastity out the way and strode over to his massive walk-in closet. "Wanna go shopping today?"

"Hell, I'm never going to say no to shopping."

"You got a passport?" Hunter asked as he picked out a shirt and matching pants.

"Yeah, why?"

"Cause I got some business to take care of in the Cayman Islands. You can go shopping while I make my moves. Then I figure we'll spend the night there, hop a flight to the Bahamas in the morning, and we'll do up Paradise Island. Come back Tuesday or Wednesday."

"Uh . . ." Chastity hesitated. "And what kind of business do you have to take care of?"

"Don't worry, I ain't gonna be carrying nothing but some cash."

"Okay," Chastity said slowly. "Because I'm not trying to go down like that."

"What do you mean?" Hunter said as he sat on the side of the bed.

"Well, you know, I know what you're into and all that, but I'm not the kind of chick who's going to take a route for you. I think we need to be straight on that up front. I don't carry drugs."

Hunter snorted. "Did I ask you to?"

"Well, no, but –"

"And I never will, ma," Hunter said, his voice suddenly serious. "I don't believe in that shit. Girl, I'm trying to make you my woman, I don't need a mule. The fuck I look like asking some female I care about to carry some shit that could her ass locked up for life?"

"Yeah," Chastity said in a soothing voice, afraid that she has pissed him off, "but it's just that a lot of guys who are dealing expect their woman to –"

"Those are some bitch niggas," Hunter said, cutting her off again. "They don't really give a shit about their women. You think them niggas talking about they want a woman who's a 'ride or die bitch' would ask their *mother* to take a route for them?"

"Shit, I would hope not," Chastity laughed, hoping to lighten the mood.

"Yeah, well, I wouldn't ask my mother or my woman to do some shit like that. I like that you put it out there that you wouldn't do it, ma, but it makes me feel bad that you felt you had to." Hunter paused, then

122

shrugged and shook his head. "Fuck it, we still gettin' to know each other. But you'll learn how I roll."

Chastity fell silent, not knowing what to say.

"Like I said, I'm going down there with a bunch of cash. I gotta make a deposit and do some face-to-face with some bankers to make sure they're taking care of my shit right," Hunter said as he slipped on a pair of socks. "You down or what?"

"Yeah, I'm down. I've never been to the Cayman Islands before." Chastity said, sitting down on the bed next to him.

"Word? I woulda bet you a high-class chick like you was well-traveled."

"Don't be trying to play me, boy. I didn't say I've never been anywhere, I just said I've never been to the Cayman Islands." Chastity started counting off on her fingers. "I've been to France, England, Egypt, Japan, Hong Kong –"

Hunter mugged her in the face, pushing her down on the bed. "Okay, okay, stop showing off."

Chastity grinned. "Hey, Hunter."

"Yeah," Hunter said as he bent down to tie his shoes.

Chastity lifted her hips up in a provocative manner. "Money ain't the only thing that can make me cum."

"Oh no?" Hunter said, the lust evident in his eyes as he looked at Chastity's perfect body. "What else turns you on?"

Chastity took his hand and moved it down to her already moist pussy. "Here, let me show you."

"Aw yeah, ma," Hunter said in a husky voice. "That's what I'm talkin' 'bout." He reached over and started massaging her breasts with one hand, while his

other immediately moved to her pelvic. He parted the lips of her pussy, and smiled at the wetness. "Yeah, that's just what I'm talkin' 'bout." He kissed her on the mouth, then slowly started kissing her from her throat, down the middle of her chest, to her stomach, and was just reaching the tip of her pubic hair, when all of a sudden the ringing of a telephone filled the room.

Hunter quickly made a move to get up, but just as quickly Chastity closed her legs around his waist, as she tried to lure him into continuing. "Let it ring, Hunt. You got some business to take care of, daddy."

To her surprise, Hunter moved with a quickness, freeing himself and reaching behind a lamp on the nightstand to pick up a cell phone that Chastity had not seen before.

"Yeah, what's up?" he said, moving toward the bathroom without even looking at Chastity, who had propped herself up on her elbows and was watching him in surprise. Her mouth dropped open as he closed the bathroom door behind him. *What the fuck?*

She lay there for a moment, trying to figure out what was going on and even considered going over to the bathroom door to try and eavesdrop, but then she heard water roaring from the sink faucet – Hunter was obviously taking precautions against just that move.

Hunter finally emerged from the bathroom a few minutes later, a pensive look on his face, and seemed to have forgotten Chastity's existence as he moved towards the bedroom window.

"So, what, you got some bitch calling you on a secret celly?" Chastity said, getting up from the bed.

"Huh?" Hunter seemed shaken by the sound of her voice. His face quickly formed an innocent

expression. "Damn, ma, you trippin'. That was just some business I had to take care of."

"Really?" Chastity walked over and got in Hunter's face. "Why didn't they call you on your iPhone, then? Is this the phone you give your ho's or your booty calls?"

"Shit," Hunter slapped her playfully on the ass, "I got all the booty I need right here."

"Then what was the call about? And how come you had to take it in the bathroom?" Chastity continued to challenge him. "You didn't want your ho to know you had a female up in here?"

"Ain't that some shit? I got me a jealous woman." Hunter laughed, and tried to pull Chastity into his arms, but she took the opportunity to grab the cell phone out of his hand. She darted toward the bathroom, hoping to slam the door before Hunter could grab her so she could have the opportunity to look through the numbers on the phone, but he was too quick. But instead of trying to playfully wrestle the phone from her, he squeezed her wrist until she was forced to drop it.

"Damn," Chastity, said as she rubbed her wrist. "You didn't have to hurt me. Is the bitch calling you worth all that?"

"I told you it wasn't any bitch," Hunter said gruffly as he picked up the phone. "Stop trippin."

Tears sprung to Chastity's eyes, tears she didn't want Hunter to see. "Fuck it," she said angrily. "I don't give a shit anyway. I'm out, nigga."

She quickly started putting on her clothes, deciding to shower when she got home rather than spend another moment in Hunter's house.

"Aw, Chas, don't be like that. I'm sorry if I hurt you, but I told you to stop playin'." Hunter said moving

behind her and grabbing her into a hug. "Why you trippin', girl? You know I ain't fucking with no one but you."

"I don't care if you are," Chastity said as she buttoned her blouse.

"Yes you do," Hunter said, rubbing her stomach and breasts. "Chastity is jealous. Chastity is jealous," he chanted in a playful voice.

"I am not!"

"Yes, you are!"

"No, I just think it's disrespectful of you to be talking to some other bitch while I'm laying naked in your bed," she said, finally wiping the tears from the corners of her eyes. "You ain't see me answering my cell while we've been together. I would never do that shit to you."

"Okay, look, how about this?" Hunter released her, then dropped the cell phone on the phone and stomped on it until it was in pieces. "See? Now if that was my ho phone can't no ho call me on it now."

Chastity crossed her arms defiantly. "Big shit. You'll just get another one."

Hunter sighed. "How about this, I promise I won't buy another cell phone without you knowing about it first, and I promise I'm not giving my number to any bitches. You the only female gonna have my number."

Chastity looked at him doubtfully. "You swear?" She finally asked.

Hunter raised up his right hand. "I swear on my mother's grave," he said solemnly.

"I didn't ask you to do all that," Chastity said. "I just want –"

"And I just want you to know how serious I am," Hunter stroked Chastity's face, his fingers trailing the wetness on her cheek. "I really am sorry if I hurt you. I swear it wasn't my intention, ma."

She sighed and snuggled up against his chest. "Don't worry, I've already figured out a way for you to make it up to me."

"How's that?"

She started unbuttoning her blouse and moving backwards toward the bed. "Come see for yourself," she said with a seductive smile.

"Yeah, ma," Hunter grinned. "That's what I'm talkin' 'bout."

"I'm telling you, Jackie, I've seen money before, but I ain't never seen that much money at one time," Chastity said on the phone in her apartment while packing her Louis Vuitton overnight bag. "He had two suitcases full; wrapped up stacks of twenties and fifties. There had to be a two or three hundred grand in each bag. Maybe more."

"Goddamn! He's pushin' it like that?"

"Yeah, bitch. And he's packing too."

"Whatchoo mean? He's traveling with irons?"

"No, I mean he's working with a big fat nine inch dick, and damn if he don't know how to use it. I ain't never cum so much in my life." Chastity giggled. "I'm telling you, Jackie. A bitch is in love."

"Oh yeah? You ain't fiendin' over Legend no more, huh?"

127

Shay

"Fuck you, ho," Chastity said, suddenly realizing that she had stopped comparing Hunter to Legend after their first night together.

"Hell, I don't give a shit." Jackie gave a little laugh. "All I wanna know is when you gonna put me down. I know the nigga must have some friends he be rollin' with. Hook a bitch up."

"Well, I haven't met any yet, and he seems like the kind of nigga who doesn't really have any close friends, but I'll keep my eyes open for you," Chastity said while getting her passport out of her bureau drawer. "Too bad you're not home, though. I wanted you to meet him."

"Shit, you betta be glad I'm not, 'cause I woulda pulled the nigga."

"Bitch, you would have tried." Chastity laughed. "But look, I'm outta here. He's going to be picking me up to go to the airport in a few minutes. And remember, don't breathe a word of this to Legend."

"Just bring me back a nigga with a bankroll and my lips are sealed forever."

Damn, Chastity thought after they hung up, *I wonder if my cell will work in the Cayman Islands. I don't want to miss Daddy's call tomorrow.* She glanced at her calendar and realized she was scheduled to meet with his lawyer on Thursday. *Good. We'll be back by then.*

Chapter Eight

"You tired of me yet?" Hunter asked while stroking Chastity's hair as she lay her head in his lap during the limousine ride home from the airport.

"No," Chastity said lazily. "You bored with me yet?"

Hunter shook his head. "You know we've only known each other . . . what . . . a week? . . . and I've spent more time with you than I've ever spent with any woman besides my mother, and I swear for shit, Chas, I don't think I'll ever be able to get enough of you. You got a nigga whipped for real."

Chastity pulled his hand to her lips and kissed it. "I feel the same way, Hunt. Kinda scary, ain't it?"

"Yeah, kinda."

They rode in silence for the next ten minutes until the limousine pulled into Hunter's driveway. He helped her out of the car, then slung two bags of luggage over his shoulder, and led her into the mansion; the chauffer following with the rest of the luggage. And there was a lot. Hunter's business had taken longer than he expected, and so Chastity's shopping spree was more even extended than she had originally hoped. And more lucrative. On the plane Hunter told her that she could spend up to five percent of the money he was planning on banking. She had figured that would be $30,000 since she estimated the cash in the bags was about $600,000,

but when he picked her up to take her to the airport he had even more bags with him; having obviously made stops to pick up money from his various spots. They were traveling with a cool $3 million. She managed to spend her total $150,000 trip allowance in a matter of hours; and had the jewelry, clothes and accessories to prove it.

Chastity sighed as she sank down on the couch. It had been helluva of a trip, and while she may not have been tired of Hunter, she was tired. She considered taking a cab home to her apartment back in Manhattan, then figured she might as well as stay one more night with her man. Because she had definitely decided he was her man; she couldn't deny the feelings she had caught feelings for him. Whenever he walked in the room her face lit up, and what was so great his face always lit up when he saw her, too. The only thing better than falling in love, she decided, was having the person you're falling in love with falling for you at the same time.

"You wanna go out for dinner? Or should I order in?" Hunter asked as he armed the security alarm after the driver left.

"Yeah, let's order in. Something light, though. I'm not too hungry. A salad will do me fine."

"Shit, girl, don't tell me you're watching your weight," Hunter said as he picked up the remote and flicked on the 52-inch plasma television. "With all the fucking we've been doing I know you've lost 20 pounds just over the week."

"I didn't hear you complaining," Chastity said, pulling him down onto the couch next to her.

"And you ain't gonna! Hell, I'm in pig's heaven." Hunter grinned. "Oink, oink."

RAW

"You are so stupid, boy," Chastity giggled, punching him in the arm.

Ding dong

"You expecting someone?" Chastity asked.

"Nope," Hunter used the television remote to switch to channel 952, and a live video picture of the outside of the mansion appeared, and Chastity saw a man in a Federal Express uniform standing at the front door with a small package in his hand.

Hunter hurried over and disarmed the security alarm again, then opened the door.

"Package for Mr. Hunter Foster," the delivery man said, handing it to him as he spoke. "No signature required.."

Hunter nodded, reached into his pocket and gave the man a tip, then closed the door and put the package down in a chair and rejoined Chastity on the couch.

"Aren't you even going to open it?" Chastity asked. "It might be important."

"Not as important as you," Hunter said, giving her a quick kiss on the forehead.

"Listen, Hunter, I'm going to have to go home tomorrow. Cool?" Chastity rubbed his thigh. "I've got to take care of some things."

"Uh huh . . . like moving out, right?" Hunter said casually.

"What?"

"Like moving out your and moving in here," Hunter used the remote to flip through the television channels again, though it was obvious he wasn't paying attention to the television screen. "I told you before I don't want no other nigga to be putting you up in his shit. Let him move his next bitch in."

"Oh? So you think it's like that, huh?"

131

"Yeah. And if you don't wanna move in here I'll get a nice apartment in the city for you. Hell, I was thinking of buying a condo, anyway, for investment purposes. You can move in there."

Chastity rolled her eyes. "Well, aren't you sweet? And I bet if I asked you'd even buy a beauty salon and let me run that, too." Chastity sucked her teeth.

Hunter turned and looked at her. "What's your problem?"

"Well," Chastity sat up on the couch. "Just so you know, I'm not moving into any condo, co-op, house, or apartment that's in someone else's name. I like owning my own shit."

"Get the fuck . . . " Hunter actually dropped the remote. "You mean to say that condo in that Fifth Avenue building is in your name? You bought that shit?"

"I didn't say all of that," Chastity said huffily. "Yeah, someone bought it for me, but you best believe it's my name, and mine is the only name on the deed."

"Yeah, but the dude who bought it is paying your mortgage, right?" Hunter persisted.

"No, he bought it for me free and clear. I don't have a mortgage note," Chastity said proudly. "All he pays for is the maintenance fee, which is only four grand a month. And even that shit is paid up for the next two years."

"Oh, you got it like that, huh?"

"Hell, yeah, I do. I know too many bitches who're homeless because some man got tired of them. That shit won't ever happen to me. God bless the child that's got his own."

Hunter was quiet for a moment. "What about your ride? That's in your name, too?"

Chastity nodded. "And I don't have a car note." She laid back on the couch, crossing her arms and looking at him. "I don't play that shit."

"You got it like that, huh?" Hunter looked at her moment, then shook his head. "Go ahead, ma. I ain't mad atcha. In fact, I'm kinda impressed. How'd a young girl like you know how to cover her ass like that?"

"Your cousin," Chastity answered. "He schooled me on a bunch of stuff when it comes to men. What to do to get them, and what to do get the most out of them. But most importantly, how not to get played by them." She shrugged. "And what can I say? I'm a quick study."

"So," Hunter said slowly. "You been trying the stuff you learned out on me?" He turned around and looked at her pointedly. "Tell me the truth."

Chastity bit her lip, as she thought about how she would answer. It was her telling the truth that had just forced the question she'd wanted to avoid in the first place. She'd told him too much of her personal business, already. But then again, if she was really considering building a life with this man, then shouldn't they be honest with each other? She took a deep breath.

"No, Hunter, I've never played you. Never." She sat back up and grabbed his hands. "I'm not mad at you for asking me that, but let me continue to be honest. That shit hurt. You've treated me as good as anyone has ever treated me, and better than most. I'm not going to lie, I enjoy all the things you bought me, but I never expected you to do shit for me, okay? Let's be clear, you did it on your own." She pulled his face toward her so that they were looking at each other straight in the eyes. "So, then let me ask you something, now. You'd only known me

133

for a few hours before you dropped almost a hundred grand on me. Why'd you do that?"

"Because . . . " Hunter hesitated.

"Because it was part of your game, right?" Chastity finished for him. "You wanted to impress me and you did a helluva job. And I know that I'm not the first girl you took shopping –"

"Shit, you're the first one I spent that much on, though."

"And I believe that. So, why'd you do it?" Chastity asked.

Hunter shrugged, then looked away. "You were the first girl I was with that I thought was worth it," he said staring straight ahead.

"Why? I know I'm fly, but I'm betting you've been with some of the most beautiful women in New York," Chastity persisted.

"Yeah, but . . . but you're just different," Hunter said slowly. "I can't say why."

"But see, that's the thing. That's what I'm talking about, Hunter. That's the way I feel about you. I'm pretty, but I know damn well you've been with prettier women. You've got money, but I've been with men with more –"

"Oh, I doubt that," Hunter interrupted.

Chastity grinned. "Well, you shouldn't. I had it hooked up for a dude I've been messing with to buy me a Maybach next month."

"Get the fuck . . . a Maybach?"

"Uh huh," Chastity said while waving her hand dismissively. "But what I'm saying is that it's not the superficial things that we get from each other that has us feeling like we do, it's something deeper." Chastity took a deep breath. "I haven't tried to play you, Hunter. I'm

falling in love with you." She waited for a moment for him to respond, and her heart sunk when he realized he wasn't going to say anything.

"Did you hear me, Hunter?" she asked finally.

"Yeah, I heard you."

"And?" she couldn't keep the hurt out of her voice, or the tears from welling up in her eyes.

"And all I've got to say is, it's about fucking time. Shit, girl. I've been in love with you since our first night together."

Chastity jumped on him, hugging him around the neck while she showered him with kisses. "Boy, don't you ever scare me like that again."

Hunter grinned and said, "What are you doing tomorrow?"

"Like I said earlier, I have to go home. I've got to take care of some business."

"Like what?"

"Like meeting with my father's lawyer to see what's going on with his case."

"Word?" Hunter nodded. "Yeah, that shit's important. In fact I'll go with you if you want."

"Really?" Chastity said in astonishment. She'd told him about her father and his situation two days after they met, and was surprised to learn that it was he who had arranged – at Legend's request – for a C.O. at the prison to smuggle in the cell phone that allowed them their daily free telephone calls. Still, she was a little shocked, and very pleased that he was willing to make a trip to the attorney's office with her. "Yeah, that would be mad cool."

"You know what's even more cool?"

"What's that?" Chastity asked, wondering what could top Hunter offering to accompany her to the lawyer's office.

"After we leave there, we going shopping. My baby wants a Maybach? My baby's getting a Maybach. And I'll be damn if it's some other nigga gonna foot the bill."

Chastity closed her eyes and let out a soft moan. "Ooh, baby, you're gonna make me cum."

"Well, shit, girl," Hunter stood up and started unbuckling his pants, "I'd be a damn fool to let you cum by yourself."

Chastity giggled, then slid off the couch and positioned herself on her knees in front of Hunter, not waiting before he stepped out of his pants before she had his dick in her hand, and then seconds later in her mouth. She rubbed his balls and played with his navel while he slowly started thrusting into her mouth.

"Yeah, girl, suck your daddy's dick," Hunter moaned. "Take all of this shit."

Chastity obligingly moved down further on her knees, so that he could slip his dick further, past her tonsils, and into her throat. She had long since learned how to overcome the instinctive gagging reflex, and was a master at deep-throating, and she was proving it to him now, and he was going crazy at the experience.

"Damn, girl. I ain't never had nobody take all of me like this," he said as he quickened his pace. "Yeah, you the shit, for real. You like giving your daddy head?"

Instead of answering, Chastity moved her hand from his balls, to his perineum, the fleshy area between his scrotum and his anus, and gave it a little tickle, knowing it was one of the most sensitive parts of a man's body.

"Goddamn!" Hunter shouted. He gave a couple of more powerful thrusts, before shooting his load down her throat, and she rubbed his muscled thighs as she swallowed every drop. He slowly slid his dick out of her, than sank down on the couch. She stood up, licked her lips, and was about to say something when she suddenly heard:

"Good to the last drop, huh?"

The words dripped sarcasm, but the baritone voice was laced with ferocious anger, she didn't have to turn around to know it was Legend. She put her hands over her breasts, then realized she was fully clothed, though she suddenly felt completely naked.

"Legend, I –" she stopped, not knowing what to say. She looked over at Hunter who was hurriedly trying to put his pants back on while still in the sitting position on the couch.

"Yo, I ain't give you the keys to my spot so you can just walk in when the fuck you want, man," Hunter said gruffly.

Legend walked over and sat down on a chair facing them, moving the Federal Express package Hunter had placed there on the floor next to him. He glared at Hunter, though he seemed to be trying to his voice calm. "I rang the bell, but no one answered so I just used my key. But when I walked in it was easy to see why the two of you didn't hear anything." He turned his icy stare to Chastity. "I decided to just wait until you were finished, Chas, I didn't want to make myself a nuisance by interrupting. Just trying to display good manners; though I'm not sure the proper etiquette in a situation like this."

"Ha, ha," Chastity said weakly. "Very funny."

Shay

"Extremely funny," Legend said with a sneer. "I'm just bursting with laughter. Can't you tell?"

"What's up, yo. What you need?" Hunter said, standing up.

"It's not what I need, it's what we need," Legend said stonily. "And especially what *you* need, and that's to be about your business."

"Man, I don't know what the fuck you're talkin' 'bout. I'm 'bout my business," Hunter said angrily.

"Yeah, nigga? Well, that's not what I've been hearing." Legend snorted. "Too busy getting your dick sucked, I guess. Isn't that right, Chas?"

Chastity gasped, but before she could say anything, Hunter was in his cousin's face.

"Man, don't be talkin' to my woman like that."

Legend jumped up from his chair so quick it fell backward behind him. "Your what?"

"You heard me, muthafucka. I said, she's my woman," Hunter shouted. "Not that it's any of your fuckin' business."

"Get out my face with that bullshit." Legend used both his arms to shove Hunter back, then turned to Chastity. "You serious about this ho nigga? What the fuck are you? Stupid?"

"Look, Legend," Chastity said moving toward him, "I know you're upset, but Hunter and I –"

"You don't have to explain shit to this muthafucker," Hunter shouted, getting in Legend's face again. "And don't put you hands on me again, you pussy bitch."

"Or what?" Legend said, not giving an inch.

"Try me, nigga, and find out," Hunter shot back. "I'll kick your ass like I used to back in the day, bitch."

Legend gave Hunter an incredulous look, then said, "Fuck it. Let's get it popping."

"No!" Chastity said, rushing to get between them, but before she could Legend threw a haymaker that landed solidly on Hunter's jaw. Then, to her horror, the two men were in a knock down drag out brawl, smashing into furniture, and slamming each other into walls, and raining each other with a series of punches and kicks.

"Stop it! Stop it!" Chastity screamed at the top of her voice as the plasma television detached from the wall and went crashing to the floor. The two men ignored her as they continued their fight. Not knowing what else to do, she tried to squeeze between them, and received a powerful and painful blow to her head for her effort. She didn't know who had hit her, and she didn't know if it was on purpose, all she knew was that all of a sudden she was seeing stars. She blacked out. When she awoke she was lying on the floor, and Legend was kneeling over her, patting her on the cheek as if trying to bring her back to consciousness.

"What happened?" she asked groggily.

"Chas, I'm sorry. I didn't mean to hit you," Legend said in a panicked voice. "Are you okay?"

"Move out the way." Hunter was suddenly bending over her; placing a wet towel on her head. "You all right, girl? Damn, I'm sorry. Please tell me you're okay."

Chastity tried to sit up, but groaned as a wave of pain swept over her.

As if working in tandem, Hunter jumped up and righted the couch, which has been overturned in the fight, and Legend tenderly scooped her up from the floor and lay her on it.

Shay

"I'm fine," Chastity said, rubbing her forehead. A knot was already beginning to form. "I'll be fine."

"You sure, ma?" Hunter's voice was full of unconcealed concern.

"Chas, I think we should get you over to a hospital and let a doctor check you out," Legend said. "You might have a concussion or something."

"Man, why don't you just get the fuck outta here and let me take care of my woman?" Hunter snapped.

"Fuck you with that 'my woman,' shit," Legend shouted. "I been taking care of young girl long before she knew your funky ass."

"Yeah, well, I got –"

"Oh, God! Would you two please just stop!" Chastity sat up on the couch. "What the fuck is wrong with you the both of you?" Just speaking made the throbbing in her head hurt even more. She groaned and lay down again. "Damn!"

"Don't worry, we're not going to start fighting again," Legend said angrily. "Shit, what's up in here worth fighting about anymore?"

She wasn't quite sure why, but his words hurt her even more than the blow to her head. She watched helplessly, not knowing what to say, as he stomped toward the door.

"Yeah, nigga, get the fuck on outta here," Hunter said with a snarl. "Coming in here like a pussy ass –"

Legend's hand was already on the door knob, but he suddenly swung around to face Hunter, and to Chastity's shock, she could see tears in his eyes.

"Hunt, man, you know in all of our fucking lives, I never . . . NEVER . . . asked you to lay off a woman. And the one time I ask, this is how you do me?

140

Damn, cuz," he said in a broken voice. "I expected more from you than this shit. You wanted to hurt a nigga you sure found the way."

"Legend, man," Hunter's voice softened. "I never meant to . . . man, I didn't know . . . shit, man. It ain't what you think. Me and Chas, man, we caught some feelings, and –"

Legend bit his lip, then shook his head and opened the door to leave, but accidentally kicked the Federal Express package lying on the floor. He picked it up and tossed it over to Hunter. "Man, like I said, you need to be handling your business. I got a phone call from our old friend. You need to be making some moves. That's all I came over here to tell you, cuz. That's all."

"Legend, wait." Hunter said, slowly standing up.

"Man, ain't shit else we got to say each other." Legend said just before walking out the door. "Fuck you, and fuck your bitch, too."

Chastity jumped up from the couch, and before Hunter could stop her she was out the door, running barefoot towards Legend. She reached him just as he was preparing to climb into his car.

"No," she said crying, and tugging at his arm. "You can't just –"

"Let go, Chas." Legend tried to shake her off.

"I can't, Legend," she said hysterically through her tears. "I can't let you go. Not like this."

"Yeah? Seems to me this is the way you wanted it, Chas." He opened the car door, but then instead of climbing in, he slammed the fist down on the roof of the car, leaving a noticeable dent. "Why, Chas? Just tell me why!"

"Legend, it's not my fault," Chastity cried. "You never told me –"

"Tell you? Girl, haven't I always shown you?" Legend said, his voice cracking. "Fuck a tell." He slammed his fist down on the car again. "Damn."

"Oh, God, Legend. I'm sorry. I'm so sorry," Chastity leaned into him, smothering her face into his chest as she continued to sob. "It's not fuck a tell. You should have said something. You should have let me know."

Legend tried to push Chastity away from him, but she clung to his neck, refusing to move. He finally hugged her, and buried his face in her hair. "Chas, tell me the truth. Do you love him? Are you in love with Hunter?"

Chastity didn't hesitate. She owed him the truth. "Yes," she wailed. "I do. But –"

"Shh," he said softly. "That's all I needed to know." He held her for a few more seconds, then gently pulled her face up so that she was looking him in the eyes. "Go ahead and do you, girl. But listen, if it doesn't work out . . . for whatever reason . . . I want you to bring your young ass home where you belong. Hear me?"

"Legend, I –"

Before she could finish, he bent his head down and kissed her softly on the lips, then kissed her again more forcefully, thrusting his tongue into her mouth and hugging her so tightly she could feel his wildly beating heart. Then he let her go, stroked her cheek one last time, and hopped in his car and sped off, tires squealing.

She stood in the driveway crying for a few minutes, before slowly making her way back into the house. She found Hunter sitting on the couch, the opened Federal Express package opened next to him, but

the contents missing. Hunter looked up when he saw her, then looked down quickly and shook his head.

"I'm sorry, ma," he said softly. He rubbed his hands over his eyes. "Things have gotten really fucked up."

Chastity nodded, as she sat down next to him. "Yeah, they have. They really have."

Chapter Nine

"**D**addy, I'm serious! If this pans out the attorney thinks it's a sure thing that we'll win your appeal," Chastity said into her iPhone as she lay, fully clothed, on Hunter's bed. "And he's talking not just getting you off of death row, but maybe even winning you a new trial!"

"Chas, honey, are you sure?" Mr. Jones asked. "I mean, why hasn't Gephardt contacted me?"

"Because he just found out the new information yesterday, Daddy. I met with him right after I got off the telephone with you, and he said he had to check on a few things, but I bet he'll be calling or coming to see you on Monday. And you know I'm going to be coming up to see you next Sunday." Chastity paused. "And, Daddy, I'm going to be bringing a friend with me, if that's okay."

"Who?" Mr. Jones asked. "Jackie? Or do I finally get to meet your mystery man, Legend?"

"Uh, no, Daddy. Actually, um, I'm going to be bringing up my boyfriend. I've told him about you, and he really wants to meet you."

"Boyfriend? What boyfriend?"

"His name is Hunter, Daddy," Chastity answered. "Hunter Foster. Make sure you put his name on the visitor's list."

"Foster? Isn't that your friend Legend's last name? Are they related?"

"Yes." Chastity sighed. She had anticipated the question. "He and Legend are cousins."

"Really? And how does Legend feel about all this?"

"He doesn't have a damn thing to do with it," Chastity snapped before she could catch herself.

"Hold on, what did you say, young lady?"

"Daddy, I'm sorry. I'm just kind of sensitive on the subject," Chastity said quickly. "I didn't mean to be rude."

"And anyway," Mr. Jones continued. "Don't you think you're too young to have a steady boyfriend? You're only nineteen. You should still be playing the field. Experiencing life. Not tied down at your age." Mr. Jones sighed. "Hell, you should be in college, meeting new and exciting people. I know Legend got you that fancy job as a PR consultant, but –"

"Daddy," Chastity said gently, "we've been over this, remember? I do plan on going to college. Hopefully, Fordham University. But right now, I want to work and save money for tuition and . . . and other things."

"Other things like spending thousands of dollars on my lawyers." Mr. Jones gave a sad chuckle. "I worked hard all my life to support my family. I never thought the day would come that I would be living off my daughter."

"Daddy, I don't mind," Chastity said firmly. "You're the most important thing in my life. Besides," she said in a lighter voice. "Soon as you get out I'm going to make sure you pay me back every dime. There, does that make you happy?"

Shay

Mr. Jones laughed. "That's my girl. Keep hope alive."

"Always, Daddy."

"Well, it's time for me to go," Mr. Jones said. "I'll put your friend's name on the list, it should clear by the time you guys drive out here next weekend. And I'll give you a call the same time tomorrow, okay?"

"Okay, Daddy. I love you."

"I love you, too, baby. Tell Jackie and Legend I said hello. And tell your so-called boyfriend he'd better treat you right or I'm going to bust out of this joint and kick his butt."

Chastity laughed. "Okay, Daddy. Bye."

Tell Legend 'hello,' he'd said. She fingered the buttons on her cell phone, considering if that would be a good enough excuse tocall Legend. It had been eight days since the confrontation at Hunter's house, and there were so many times she wanted to pick up the telephone and give him a call, but she'd always change her mind. Partly because she wasn't sure if he'd take her call and if he did how he would act. And partly because she didn't want to cause him any further pain; not that she wasn't hurting herself. As much as she loved Hunter, Legend had been her friend, confidant, and mentor for three years – and she missed him sorely. She'd never before gone a whole week without at least a phone message from him.

Her relationship with Hunter had also undergone a change. He was more attentive and loving than ever when he was around her, but the problem was he was seldom around during the day. Whatever business it was that Legend had alluded to seemed to be taking most of Hunter's time, though he made sure to check in with her two or three times day, assuring her that he loved her,

and also inquiring if she'd heard anything from Legend. He'd also given her his key and the code for his security alarm, encouraging her to spend as much as time as she liked at his house. She readily complied, since he did manage to make it home every night, and they could spend a little time together.

It was during some of their late night conversations that she learned more about Hunter and Legend's early family life. Hunter told her that his and Legend's fathers had been brothers, though Legend's was the more successful in business. Neither had been to college, but Legend's father went into real estate, eventually becoming a broker, and was able to eke out a middle-class living. Hunter's dad, on the other hand, worked as a security guard at a supermarket. Steady work, but not well-paying. The two brothers remained close, and the two families were always welcome in each other's houses, though Hunter's dad was always too proud to ever accept any financial help. There were times, Hunter told her, that they went days with the gas and electricity turned off because they were unable to pay the bills.

After Hunter's parent died and he went to live with his aunt and uncle, his life improved vastly, but he'd never forgotten those lean times. Lean times that Legend never knew first-hand.

Though Hunter hated gangs since his father died in the crossfire between the Crips and the Bloods, he started selling drugs – cocaine – for an independent dealer when he was seventeen. He moved out on his own a few months later, and Legend was a frequent visitor to his new apartment and house-sat for him when he went on occasional trips to New York on behalf of his employer. It was during one of these trips that Hunter

Shay

was able to make his own connection with a small but organized drug ring operating out of Harlem and headed by a cat named Jeezy.

"I started making some moves, and in a couple of years I was doing okay," Hunter explained. "I never worked a corner, I'd done that shit in L.A. Here, in New York, I was one of the niggas who had workers posted up. After I started making a couple of thousand a week, I convinced Legend he should come up and check out the East Coast. He'd started fuckin' around, dealing and shit, while I was gone, and I told him he could move up faster in the game here in New York."

Hunter had immediately put Legend down when he arrived, and the two of them were making moves. Within months of Legend's arrival both were involved in the inner-workings of the organization. But then shit started falling apart, Hunter told Chastity. Workers were getting busted, spots were being raided, and Jeezy, started looking at everyone crossed-eyed, figuring he had to have a narc in his operation. At the same time he was warring with a former partner who'd gone out on his own, so the operation had workers being busted by cops, and killed by Jeezy's drug rival. Then some serious shit went down, Hunter wouldn't tell Chastity exactly what, but soon Hunter and Legend had their own drug operation. And they no longer had workers on the street.

"Shit, we were the suppliers, the people getting the shit right off the boat. We were the ones selling the weight to the dealers who had workers on the street. Shit was sweet," Hunter's eyes lit up as he spoke. "We went from making a couple of thousand a week to making a couple ten thousand a week."

As soon as Legend had banked a million dollars in overseas accounts he told Hunter he wanted out of the

148

life. He'd already started giving his exclusive parties, and there was more than enough money in that business to keep him satisfied.

"But me, naw, ma . . . I guess I'm greedy. Or maybe I still ain't forgot what it's like not to have shit," Hunter told her with a shrug. "You know as hard as my father worked all them years on his job his company insurance was barely enough to cover his burial expenses. If Uncle Luther hadn't ponied up some paper, my mom and dad woulda just about been buried in a fuckin' pine box. That's some fucked up shit. That shit won't ever happen to me and mine."

Still, Hunter told her, lately he'd been thinking maybe it was time for him to retire. He didn't say why, but Chastity knew it had something to do with the cryptic message Legend had delivered about handling his business.

The ringing of her telephone brought Chastity out of her musings about her conversations with Hunter. She looked down and saw it was Jackie calling.

"Hey, girl."

"God damn it, Chas, if you ain't never gonna be home why don't you just let me move into your shit?"

"How do you know I'm not home?" Chastity said, getting up from the bed and stretching.

"Cause I been over here for the last hour watching *All My Children* and eating popcorn, is how, ho."

Jackie was never one to ever really be in a pleasant mood, but she really seemed to be in full bitchy mode at the moment, Chastity noted. "Yeah? What's Erica Kane up to these days?"

"Bitchy as ever," Jackie snapped. "When you bringing your ass home?"

"I don't know. I'll probably stop through there tomorrow some time. I'm just gonna chill over here today."

"Here bein' Hunter's crib?" Jackie sucked her teeth. "Yeah, you done forgot about a bitch now that you're living in the lap of luxury."

"Shut up, Jackie. I was living in the lap of luxury right there in my own apartment, too."

"Yeah, well then come on home to it. A bitch been missin' ya, Chas. Shit." Jackie sucked her teeth again. "And you been fuckin' around with Hunter for weeks now, and I still ain't even met his ass. I'm beginning to wonder if he even fuckin' exists."

"I know how to prove it," Chastity said with a smile. "How about I pick you up tomorrow around three and I take you to shopping over at Bloomingdales or Saks? Hunter gave me his platinum American Express Card to keep me company while he's taking care of his business."

"Uh huh, see now you talkin' a bitch's language," Jackie said gleefully. "And how 'bout we stop by Tiffany's or Harry Winston's so you can hook me up with a nice piece of ice?"

Chastity shrugged, "Yeah, we can do that. I want to get a new bracelet anyway."

"Bet. I'ma see you at three tomorrow, then, and your ass best not be late."

"I love you too, ho," Chastity said, before hanging up. It had been a minute since she'd spent any real time with Jackie, so she was already looking forward to their shopping trip the next day.

She was contemplating which store to stop by first when she heard the front door open downstairs. She

glanced at the clock. It was barely 3 p.m. "Hunter?" she called out.

"Yeah!"

Chastity got up and walked to the top of the stairway, calling out, "Well, this is a pleasant surprise. I'd almost forgotten what you looked like in the daylight."

She was getting ready to walk down the stairs when she saw that Hunter was not alone. There were at least four or five other men, no five or six, she noted, milling around the living room, all were huge, bigger even then Hunter, and all wearing dark sunglasses and grim faces.

"Stay up there a minute, Chas," Hunter said as he jogged up the stairs toward her. "I gots to talk to you."

She followed him back to the bedroom. "What's going on," she asked suddenly frightened.

"Sit down a minute," Hunter said motioning toward the bed. "Look," he said when she was seated. "Some real fucked up shit is going down." He leaned one arm on the dresser as if propping himself for some kind of moral support. "Chas, two of my men were blown away this afternoon."

"What!" Chastity jumped off the bed. "When? How? Hunter, are you hurt?"

Hunter shook his head. "Naw, ma. I wasn't there when it happened. No one, was. Their bodies were found in their cars in two different locations, spots where whoever shot them knew they'd be found. Both of them were shot in the back of the head, execution style."

"Oh, my God," Chastity sank back down.

Shay

"They were some good niggas, Chas." Hunter shook his head. "And they both had families. Shit is fucked up."

Chastity nodded, trying to take it all in. "Do you have any idea who did it?" she asked softly.

"Yeah, I gots me a good idea, and the muthafucka is gonna pay. But right now I got to make some serious moves, ma. And I can't do that unless I know you're safe."

Chastity's head jerked back. "You think someone would come after me to get to you?" Her heart started beating rapidly. In the back of her mind she'd known there was a risk dealing with a drug dealer, but she'd managed to convince himself that at the level Hunter was dealing, the risk would be minimal. Now she could see just how wrong she was.

"I don't think so, ma," Hunter said slowly. "In fact, I would bet against it. But I'm just not willing to take a chance. If something happened to you I'd be going to Iran somewhere to get the fuckin' atomic bomb to drop on their asses. I need to take you somewhere safe where you can lay low."

"Can't I just go to my apartment?" Chastity asked in a trembling voice. "No one knows where I live."

"I'm pretty sure no one does, and word, no one even knows of any connection between us." Hunter paused. "No one but Legend, and you know he ain't sayin' shit to nobody."

Chastity nodded.

"But again, I just don't wanna take any chances, Chas. I got a place over the bridge in Jersey that I'm gonna have two of my boys take you to. They'll be staying there with you, just in case any funky shit jumps

off. You might have to stay up there a couple of days, a week at the most, until I get shit straight."

"What?" Chastity's mind started racing furiously. Everything was happening so fast. Not ten minutes before she was making plans to go shopping the next day with her best friend; now plans were being made for her to be spirited away to God knows where for God knows how long so that God knows who didn't blow her brains out for God knows what. How the hell had she gotten herself in a situation like this, she wondered. And, more importantly, how the hell was she going to get herself out?

"Chas, are you listening to me?" Hunter said impatiently.

"Yeah, yeah," Chastity said quickly. "But Hunter, I really would feel safer in my own apartment. I've got a doorman, and there's 24-hour security –"

"Girl, listen to me. If someone wants to get at you, fuck a doorman and your building's rent-a-cop security guards, they're gonna get at you. Let me do this my way," Hunter pleaded. "I know what I'm doin', ma. The guys working for me? They're glocks stay on ready, and they know to bust a cap in a nigga and ask questions later. You feel me?"

Chastity didn't know what else to do but to nod her head, once again, in agreement.

"Good, now come here a minute. I need to show you something." Hunter extended his hand, and then led her to the window. He pulled the curtains back, then bent down over the huge air conditioning unit, and removed the front. The unit was huge, at least 3 foot in length, and five feet in width. To Chastity's astonishment, she realized it was actually a safe.

Hunter smiled at the expression on her face. "Yeah, see, anyone looking at it wouldn't suspect shit, but the air conditioning unit is only the top part where the vents are. I like to keep cool cash." He grew serious again. "Okay, the code for the safe is –"

"Wait, don't I need to write this down?"

Hunter shook his head. "Naw. The code is 10-22-19-82. You can remember that, right?"

"Yeah," Chastity said softly. "I can remember that." After all, it was Legend's birthday. October 22, 1982.

"I thought so." Hunter punched the numbers in, then opened the safe door. Chastity gasped. There were piles and piles of money neatly stacked up inside. Hunter took out half of one the stacks, and handed the cash to Chastity. "That's fifty thousand dollars. I want you to take it with for just in case. Just in case what, I don't know. But just in case."

"Fifty thousand," Chastity repeated after him. She turned to look at the contents of the safe again. The money in her hands represented less than half of one of the piles of money, and there were at least fifty piles. She quickly did the math in her head. Damn. She'd been sleeping and fucking in a room with a cool five mil all that time and didn't know it. It was then that she noticed there was also a gun in the safe, but she wasn't concentrating on that. It was the money she was concerned about. "Fifty thousand for just in case."

"Right. If you find you need more, contact me and I'll get it for you, or get Rhino or Hulk to drive you over so you can get it yourself. But don't let them know where the safe is, or tell them the code. Cool?"

"Who's Rhino and Hulk?" Chastity asked.

"The two guys who are gonna be stayin' with you," Hunter said patiently. "Remember, I said I'd have —"

"Right, right, I just wasn't thinking," Chastity said quickly. "I'm going to need to stop by my apartment and get some clothes and things before we head out to New Jersey."

Hunter hesitated. "I don't think that's a good idea, ma."

"Hunter, come on now!" Chastity said, her frustration and anger finally boiling over. "You come in here talking about dead men, executioners, and putting me up in a strange house with two strangers for who knows how long, and I'm not even going to even have a change of clothes? What kind of shit is that? Shit, I need things. You expect me to send your boys out to the store to get me sanitary napkins and —"

Hunter threw his hands up in front of him, "Chas, Chas, Chas, okay, girl. Calm down. I'll have them stop you by your spot. In fact, I'll come with you. Okay? Just chill."

Chastity looked at him, the money still in her hands, and her bottom lip quivering as she fought to keep herself from surrendering to the hysterics she knew was just below the surface.

Hunter seemed to notice her emotional state for the first time, and his face softened as he led her to the bed and sat her down. "Baby, I'm really sorry to put you through all this. But I swear, I'll make it up to you, okay? But I need you to be strong up in this joint right about now." He stroked the side of her face. "Do you think you can do that for me?"

Chastity took a deep breath before answering. "Yeah, of course, Hunt. You're my nigga, and if you're

155

going through some shit, I'm going through it with you. I'm in it, babe."

Hunter smiled, "There's the young girl I know." He picked up one of her hands and kissed it. "How about we go somewhere exotic after all this shit is over? Tahiti or some fuckin' place?"

Chastity shrugged. "Sure sounds better than New Jersey."

Hunter laughed and stood up. "One more thing, though. You can't tell nobody, and I mean nobody where you are. Don't even make or accept any phone calls less it's me. That's important, because the more people who know, the more people who can be gotten to."

"I can't even tell Jackie? And what about my father?" Chastity said in a panic stricken voice. "He's going to worry if he can't reach me."

"Don't worry, I already sent word out to my boy at the prison to tell your pops that you're gonna be outta pocket for a minute. And Jackie'll live without hearing from you for a couple of days. From what you've told me she sounds like a big girl."

"Yeah, but that doesn't mean she won't be worried about me," Chastity protested.

"Not as worried as I'll be about you if you do tell her," Hunter insisted.

"Yeah, all right, whatever. When do we leave?"

"Right now! Come on down and I'll introduce you to Rhino and Hulk."

Chastity stood up, and dutifully followed Hunter out of the bedroom. "Who are all of the rest of the niggas down there?" she asked in a low voice as they walked down the stairs.

156

"Their names don't matter, ma. Two of them are going to be stickin' with me, and two more will be stayin' up in here, ready to surprise anyone who comes lookin' up in this joint for me. But as far as I'm concerned the fewer people who know you, the better."

Hunter's phone started ringing, and he answered without even first looking at the number. "Speak," he said gruffly . . . "Word? . . . Already? . . . damn, them niggas weren't playin' . . . but yeah, that's why they gettin' the big bucks . . . All right, I'll be there in a few." He snapped the phone shut.

"Chas, I'm sorry, but I hired some professionals from out-of-town to help me clean up this mess, and they got here sooner than I expected. I'm not going to be able to ride with you to your place, ma. But you'll be fine. I'll have Hulk ride with you in your wheels, and Rhino will be following you in his."

Chastity shrugged and nodded simultaneously. They had reached the bottom of the stairs when a thought suddenly stuck her. "Hunter, what about Legend? Does he know what's going on?"

"Yeah, that was him on the phone. He's got my back just like always," Hunter said with what sounded like a mixture of pride and amazement. "He didn't even need to be in this shit, but when he heard how I was in trouble, he got in the middle. But that's how Legend rolls. Loyal to the fuckin' end."

Chapter Ten

I
t only took twenty-five minutes to make it to Chastity's 5th Avenue apartment, and the man, Hulk, sitting in the driver's seat said nothing the whole ride. Which was fine with Chastity, she didn't feel like talking. She used the time to think and try to settle her nerves. She went over and over it in her mind, could she be in danger? Did anyone know about her connection to Hunter? They'd kept a low profile, at first because they didn't want Legend to find out about their relationship, and later because Hunter was so preoccupied with 'his business' that they didn't have much opportunity to go out and party. Still, if someone had been following him, or watching his house, they might have spotted her and found out who she was. She might be a target, after all. The thought brought on a violent shiver.

"You okay?" Hulk asked, looking at her through the corner of his dark sunglasses. "Want I should turn down the air?"

"No, I'm fine," Chastity answered. "Make a left here. My building's in the middle of the block.

After they pulled up, he came around and opened her door, but not before looking up and down the street, and waiting for Rhino – who had pulled up behind them, to also nod an 'all clear.'

Even at 5'10, she felt tiny standing next to them. Both appeared to about 6'6, and their names Hulk and

Rhino were good descriptions of the physiques. Big, huge even, but there didn't seem to be an inch of fat on either of them. Hulk, who seemed to be the leader of the two, was light-skinned, almost yellow, with freckles and red hair. Even his bushy uni-brow, was red. He spoke in quiet tones, and was polite, but nevertheless he was intimidating. Maybe it was his size. Maybe because she knew that he was packing a glock, and as Hunter had said, he knew what the hell to do with it.

Like Hulk, Rhino was dressed in all black, which made his dark-skin seem even darker, almost blue-black. And since his lips were almost a freakish light pink, he looked like a cartoon character. There was nothing comical about his mannerisms, though. He was constantly looking from side-to-side as they walked into the building, and Chastity greeted the doorman.

"I'm going to be just a few minutes," Chastity said during the short elevator ride up. Rhino nodded his head, but Hulk said nothing. Oh yeah, this is going to be a lively next couple of days, Chastity thought grimly as she turned her key in the door. She'd barely gotten the door opened when she heard someone singing and snapping their fingers. *Oh good, Jackie's still here.* But before Chastity could call out to greet her friend, Hulk reached behind her and pushed her into the wall, and Rhino ran into the apartment glock in hand. Before Chastity could stop him he pointed it at Jackie, who was in the corner, with a headset over her ears, eyes closed, jamming to Beyonce's latest hit. In fact, Jackie was in the middle of the Beyonce booty-roll, when she opened her eyes and saw the big black gun. She screamed and fell backwards against the wall.

"Hold up!" Chastity yelled, running forward. "She's a friend of mine!"

"What the fuck is goin' on?" Jackie shouted as she yanked off the headset and scrambled to her feet, her eyes as wide as basketballs. "Who the hell . . . what the hell . . . Chas?"

"Sorry, we didn't expect anyone to be here," Rhino said as he finally lowered the gun.

"What the fuck is goin' on?" Jackie repeated, in a lower but trembling voice. Chastity looked down and noticed a wet spot widening on her friend's white pants. Jackie had peed on herself, though she didn't seem to notice. Yet.

"It's a long story," Chastity said as she grabbed Jackie by the arm and started pulling her toward the bedroom. "Come on."

"The fuck," Jackie said when there were inside. "You got muthafuckas comin' in here with you with guns and shit? Who the fuck are they? And why the fuck are they here? Them niggas were about to bust a cap on me. The fuck!"

"Calm down, Jackie," Chastity said soothingly.

"You calm down! I wanna know what the fuck is goin' on. Who are thóse niggas?" She was about to sit down when she felt the wetness in her pants. "Damn, that nigga scared me so bad I pissed myself."

"I'm sorry about all this," Chastity said, pulling two pieces of Gucci luggage from her walk-in closet and throwing them on the bed. "Hunter's having some, um, some business problems, and he's thinks I should lay low for a minute while he takes care of them." She started packing up her lingerie and toiletries in one bag, and clothes in another. "I'm going to be out of town for a couple of days."

RAW

"Business problems? What kind of business
prob . . . oh shit!" Jackie's eyes widened. "He got
someone after him?"

"Yeah, I think so." Chastity went into the
bathroom and emerged with bumpers and a curling iron
which she threw in the toiletry bag. "And he's says he
doesn't think anyone would come at me, but he wants
me out of town just in case."

Jackie grabbed a magazine off one of the
nightstands and placed it on the chair before sitting
down. "So, where you goin?"

"To –" Chastity hesitated, remembering her
promise to Hunter's to let no one know her whereabouts.
"It's probably best you don't know, Jackie. But I'll be in
touch, I promise you."

"Why the fuck you can't tell me?" Jackie asked
accusingly. "You think I'ma be tellin' someone?"

Chastity shook her head. "Naw, Jackie. It ain't
even like that. But I promised I wasn't going to tell
anyone." Something funny hit her, and she let out a
chuckle. "Come to think of it, I don't know exactly
where I'm going. Some spot Hunter has over the
bridge."

"What about your new car? Ain't they supposed
be delivering your Maybach later this week."

"Hmph, I'm not even thinking about no wheels
at the moment, Jackie," Chastity said as zipped up the
luggage, then looked around to see if she'd forgotten
anything. "I'm worried about me, and I'm worried about
my man."

"Yeah, I'm feelin' you, Chas. Girl, I don't know
how you staying so calm with all this goin' on." Jackie
stood up as Chastity tugged the bags off the bed. "Hey,
girl, anything I can do to help?"

"Well," Chas flashed a smile. "You can grab that other bag."

Jackie snorted. "Fuck that. I know them gorillas out there gotta be good for something besides stickin' a piece in a bitch's face."

"Oh come on now, Jackie. Rhino didn't do all that." Chastity rolled her eyes. "He just pointed it at you."

"Yeah? Well, when you're on the wrong side of the gun, I'ma tell you it all feels the same." Jackie said, while patting down her weave her hair in the mirror. "But, Chas, listen." She bit her lip and turned to Chastity. "Make sure you do stay in touch and let me know what's goin' on. Okay? You like my blood, and I couldn't stand it if some shit happened to you."

Five days and counting. This shit is getting old fast. Chastity shut the book she'd been reading and looked over at Hulk and Rhino who were sitting in front of the television playing games on an Xbox like two teenagers. *If I don't get out of here soon I'm going to smash that fucking game box and smash them two niggas, too.*

Chastity sighed and got up from the couch, and admitted to herself that she was just being cranky. Hulk and Rhino had actually been nothing but perfect gentlemen, attending to her every need. Hulk, it turned out was a pretty good cook, and turned out some decent dinners. That combined with the fact that she never caught him ogling her made her wonder if maybe he was gay. Rhino, on the other hand, was giving her full the up

and down treatment whenever he thought she wasn't looking. But he never came out his mouth wrong, so she wasn't bothered. But neither had any real conversation for her, except to ask if she needed anything, and the few attempts she'd made at conversation were met with one syllable responses. She didn't know them any better than when she did when they arrived at the two-story frame house five days before. But that might have been part of the marching orders they'd gotten from Hunter, make sure she was comfortable, but leave her the hell alone. He didn't seem like the overly jealous type, but it would figure that he wouldn't want the men who were virtually living with her to get overly friendly, especially since he wasn't there to keep an eye on things.

True to his word, Hunter always managed to get at least four telephone calls into her a day, though the length of those calls varied. Sometimes he'd talk for a good twenty minutes, telling her how much he loved and missed her, how sorry he was that she had to be sent away like this, and how everything was working out fine so she'd be able to return to the city "any day now." Sometimes the calls only lasted 30 seconds because he was busy.

The house was comfortable, not as comfortable as Hunter's house in Long Island or her own apartment, but it could do in a pinch she decided when she saw it for the first time. But as time passed the pinch was fast beginning to feel a helluva a lot like a punch. *Damn, if I'm going crazy being cooped in a house for five days, imagine how Daddy feels being locked up in a prison cell for three years.* She let out a huge sigh as she thought about her father, causing Hulk to look up from the game.

Shay

"You okay?" he said, setting the controls down in his lap.

"Fine," she said. "Just a lot on my mind."

He nodded, and returned to his game, causing Chastity to roll her eyes. *I guess his duty was done just by asking.* She walked into the kitchen and poured herself a glass of orange juice, observing that the container was almost empty. Hulk had said something about going out for groceries later that day, and she made a mental note to tell him get more. She looked at the clock on the microwave. 12:55 p.m. Hunter had missed his normal noon call, and Jackie would be getting ready to get her daily fix of *All My Children.*

Normally she would be waiting on a call from her father, but even that was a no go. They hadn't been able to talk since her journey to Camden, New Jersey. She had placed a couple of calls to his attorney, Louis Gephardt, though, and he was even more optimistic than ever. It seemed that her father's first attorney, a young black man fresh out of law school was now secretly dating a judge on the New York State of Appeals. The judge was almost twice his age. The judge was married with children. The judge was white. The judge was a former prosecutor for the D.A.'s office. The judge was the one who had prosecuted her father's case.

"If we can prove that they were seeing each other while the trial was going on," Mr. Gephardt had enthusiastically told Chastity, "we can prove impropriety and conflict of interest. The case would automatically be eligible for appeal, and would be sent back for a new trial, or the sentence might be overturned all together because of impropriety, and your father freed."

The problem was proving that they were actually seeing each other during the trial. And the odds of

164

finding proof was even more difficult given the fact that Gephardt hadn't even found out about their current relationship on his own. Someone had sent a manila envelope, with no return address, with photos and a cryptic note saying "more to come." Gephardt had hired a private investigator – billed to Chastity, of course – but all he'd done was find further proof of their present relationship. Chastity knew that their greatest help would likely come from the anonymous sender of the first batch of material – a person who obviously had it in for the judge.

I might as well watch All My Children so I can have something to talk to Jackie about. As Chastity strode past the living room and upstairs to watch the television in the bedroom, she heard Hulk push his chair back and get up.

"I'm heading out to the store, man," he told Rhino. "You want anything?"

Chastity was about to shout down for him to bring back orange juice, but Rhino beat her to it.

"Yeah, we're low on O. J., and bring back a quart of vodka to go with it."

"Shit, Hunter'd have our asses if he found out we were drinking on the job," Hulk answered.

"Well, bring me back some pussy, then," Rhino grumbled. "I'm tired of beating my shit off thinking of that bitch upstairs. I ain't use to having a fine piece of ass around the house that I ain't tappin'."

Chastity gave a low chuckle as she closed her bedroom door. Nice to know I'm appreciated. She yawned and looked out the window, but all she saw was the usual. Small rundown houses with small unkempt lawns, littered with children's bikes and toys. The house she was staying was the best kept on the block, but that

165

Shay

still didn't say much considering the block. Even the cars parked in the driveways spoke of the neighborhood economics. Hyundais, Ford Escorts, and other inexpensive vehicles. It was a good thing the house they were staying in had a small garage, otherwise her Mercedes Benz would have stuck out like a sore thumb. The car Rhino had been driving, on the other hand, fit right in. A blue 1999 Toyota Corolla which had obviously seen better days. That was the one now parked in front of the house.

She plopped down on the bed, deciding to take a nap instead of watching television. That's all there is do around here, she thought as she snuggled into a pillow, talk on the phone, watch television, eat and sleep. *This shit stinks.*

She woke up a little while later when she heard a crashing sound and then shouting coming from downstairs. She jumped up, and ran into the hallway and was ready to lean over the banister to see what was going on, but then heard a gunshot. She stood paralyzed for a moment, but then ran into the hallway bathroom. Breathing heavily, she put her ear to the door.

"You got thirty seconds, Rhino, and then I'm gonna blow your fucking head off. Where is he?" shouted an unfamiliar voice.

"Fuck you," Rhino shouted back.

"You got twenty seconds, motherfucker!"

"Fuck the twenty, Dwayne," another unknown voice yelled. "This pussy gonna talk now."

Chastity almost peed her in her pants as she heard a gunshot ring out, and then Rhino howling in pain.

"You bitch! You bitch. You done shot my leg off! I'ma kill you, muthafucka!" Rhino was howling at the top of his lungs.

"I'ma shoot your dick off, next, less'en you tell where Hunter's hiding out," the taunting voice answered.

"Fuck you. It takes six of you niggas bustin' in here to take care a two niggas, and you still ain't gonna learn shit," Hulk shouted. "And John-Boy, you ain't nothing but a snitch bitch nigga. Fuck you gonna turn on Hunter after all the shit he done for you?"

"Shut the fuck up, bitch. You ain't gonna live to tell him shit," came back the taunting voice, which Chastity assumed belonged to John-Boy.

"Tell me something we don't know, you back-stabbing pussy," Hulk yelled. "Don't matter what we tell you or don't tell you we know you ain't gonna let us live. So fuck you. You wanna find Hunter? Find him your damn selves."

"Shut the fuck up, Hulk," John-Boy said. "Rhino, you wanna keep your dick? Where the fuck is Hunter?"

"Rhino, don't say shit," Hulk shouted. "He's gonna cap us any fucking way. Ain't no way John-Boy gonna let anyone live to know he's working for Wheatie. Or that he rolled up here in Danny's car, which means he's working for Wheatie, too."

"Didn't I tell you to shut the fuck up?" John-Boy yelled.

"Fuck you! Pull the trigger, bitch," Hulk shouted. "Usually you kill ho's, go ahead and learn what it feels like to kill a real man."

Chastity jumped and covered her mouth to keep herself from screaming as she heard another gunshot.

"Yo, John-Boy, next time you put a muzzle to someone's head, go ahead and shoot your shit. Don't let me be the one hafta dust a nigga."

"Fuck you, Dwayne. I was gonna do it. Either way, the nigga's dead, right?" There was a pause, then John-Boy said, "Fuck that shit Hulk was spittin', Rhino. Let us know where Hunter is and you get to hop outta here with one leg, but otherwise intact. Otherwise, you gonna join Hulk in a dirt nap."

"Go to hell," Rhino said in a pain-filled voice. "I ain't never been a snitch-nigga. I'm going out like a man."

"Well, the hell with you, then!"

There was six gunshots, and then silence.

"John-Boy, youse one stupid nigga. You shoulda capped Hulk as soon as we walked in instead of letting him talk all that shit."

"Fuck it, Dwayne," John-Boy answered. "The muthafucka's dead now, ain't he?"

"Yeah, but you shoulda shot him before he got it into Rhino's head that we was gonna kill them either way. Rhino weren't as smart as Hulk, he probably wouldn'ta figured out that shit out if Hulk ain't hipped him to it."

Chastity stood inside the bathroom paralyzed, but mentally she nodded her head, suddenly understanding. Dwayne was right. Hulk was running off with the mouth and not just to Rhino, but also to let her know the deal. He made sure to say John-Boy's and Danny's name so that she could let Hunter know they were snitches if she made it out alive. And he even gave the exact amount of niggas who were in the spot. Her heart sunk, as she remembered the remark about John-Boy only killing ho's. Hulk was letting her know that if

John-Boy found her in the house he wouldn't hesitate to kill her, too.

But that's if he found her. She ran over to the bathroom window in hopes of climbing out, but when she looked down she saw if she jumped there was nothing to break her fall. She'd wind up with a broken limb or limbs, and couldn't possibly get to her car before they caught her. Her only hope was to wait for them to leave, and then make a break for it.

She tip-toed back to the door and pressed her ear against it again.

"Come on, let's get the fuck out of here," Dwayne was saying.

"Wait a minute," John-Boy said in response.

"For what?"

"I wanna take a look around. You know that muthafucka Hunter got stacks. I wouldn't mind getting my hand on that some of that shit," John-Boy said with a laugh.

Chastity ran to the bathroom window again, and looked down in despair. She was going to have to take a chance and jump.

"The fuck is wrong with you?" Dwayne said. "You don't think someone heard all them caps flying in here? The 5-0 is probably already on the way. Let's get the fuck outta here."

"Alright, well, yo, I gotta take a piss," John-Boy said. "Let me do that real quick and then we'll bounce."

Shit, Chastity thought. Knowing that they couldn't see the bathroom door from downstairs, and hoping it wouldn't creak, she opened it a crack so that it wouldn't look suspicious, as if someone was in there. Then she jumped in the bathtub, and drew the shower curtain, holding her breath as she heard John-Boy

169

running up the stairs. But instead of entering the bathroom, he went instead to the bedroom, and she could hear him rummaging through drawers and throwing things in the floor.

"Hurry up," Dwayne called from downstairs. "We gonna leave your ass."

"Cool out, nigga. I'm coming," John-Boy shouted back.

Her heart jumped as the bathroom door flew open, actually hitting the bathtub, as she heard John-Boy come in. He was cursing under his breath as he relieved himself in the commode, then she heard the toilet flush.

"Yo, John-Boy, your cell is ringing. Will you come the fuck on?" another voice shouted out.

"I said the fuck I'm coming, nigga!" A few seconds later John-Boy was out the bathroom and running down the stairs.

She waited another ten minutes after she heard the front door slam before shakily emerging from the bathroom. She hurried into the bedroom, looking for her bag so she could retrieve her phone and call Hunter. Then remembered she'd left it downstairs in the living room next to the couch.

Her legs shook as she descended the stairs, dreading what she'd see. It was worse than what she expected. She spotted Hulk first. His body lay slumped against a radiator pipe, and as she drew closer she could see that one of his hands had been handcuffed to the pipe. Half of his head had been blown away, and bits of bone and brain matter were floating in the pool of blood. And the force of the bullet which entered the left side of his head had been enough to dislodge his right eye; it hung by bloody ligaments on his bloody cheek and seemed to be staring up at her.

But it was Rhino's body, which was tied up in a chair that was the most horrific. His face had beaten so badly that he wasn't recognizable. She didn't know what kind of gun the hoods used but it must have been high caliber; when Rhino had said they had blown his leg off he wasn't exaggerating, it lay on the floor next to the chair. The last series of shots had left his arm dangling, a gaping hole in his chest and stomach, and true to his word . . . John-Boy had taken deadly aim at Rhino's groin.

Nausea swept over Chastity as she leaned against a wall for support. As she looked around, trying to locate her bag, her stomach started rumbling, and before she could make a dash back upstairs to the bathroom she fell to her knees and vomited there on the living room floor.

She retched again as she realized she was kneeling in a pool of blood and watched, horrified, as her stomach contents mixed with blood and bone matter. She scrambled to her feet and tried to compose herself, but tears were streaming down her face. As she wiped her mouth she saw the strap of her Fendi bag peeking from under the couch. She walked over and pulled it out, wondering how'd it gotten there, then concluded that the quick thinking Hulk must have managed to kick it there so that John-Boy and his cohorts didn't realize there was another person in the house. She looked over at him gratefully, then quickly averted her eyes. She took a couple of quick deep breaths, then pulled her phone out and punched in Hunter's number. "Shit, he's not picking up. It's going straight to fucking voice mail," she said out loud before hanging up. She stood there wondering what to do next. Of course she had to get out of there, but was there anything she needed to do before she did?

Shay

Calling the police was out of the question. In fact, she thought, as she looked around again, she probably needed to remove any traces of her having been on the scene. She rushed upstairs to change her clothes and but as soon as she reached the top landing a sinking feeling overcame her. Fucking DNA. Even if the police found her fingerprints it wouldn't mean she was there when the massacre went down, but the fact that she had vomited in the blood would tie her to the scene, she knew that much from watching *CSI* on television. *Oh, God, I've got to go back and clean it up. But wait, even if they do find it, they don't have anything to match it against. I've never been arrested.* Still she knew it was better to be safe than sorry.

She went back downstairs and into the kitchen and got a plastic bag and paper towels, then slowly entered the living room again. She took a couple of deep breaths, then got on her knees and started cleaning up the vomit, trying hard not to retch again as she did so.

When she finished, she stood up and was preparing to change her clothes and split the scene when she heard a gurgling sound. She gasped as she realized it was coming from Rhino. *Oh my God, he's still alive!* She dashed to his side, and lifted his bloody head. His eyes were closed, and blood bubbled from his mouth.

"Rhino, I'ma get you to a hospital, okay?"

The blood started streaming faster from his mouth and she realized he was trying to say something. She leaned in closer, trying to make out his words, then let out a loud gasp – almost a scream – when she finally understood what he was saying: "Legend. Tell Hunt . . . John-Boy was . . . talking to . . . Legend on the phone . . . nigga . . . musta . . . ratted him out."

172

Chapter Eleven

Three-thirty, Chastity noted as she drove through the streets of Camden, heading for the New Jersey Turnpike. She still hadn't been able to reach Hunter, and even Jackie seemed to be missing in action. It wasn't like her not to answer her telephone, but every time Chastity tried her phone it would ring six times and then go to voice mail. She even texted her, simply punching in 911, but her friend still hadn't gotten back to her.

Rhino had to be wrong, she thought as she wiped tears from her eyes with one hand as she drove. *There was no way Legend would turn on his cousin. But then again, would he? Could he have been that fucked up about me and Hunter hooking up?* She tried to push the thought out of her head, trying to convince herself again that Rhino was mistaken, but in her heart she knew the truth.

With Legend on their side it was just a matter of time before they tracked down Hunter, especially if he still didn't know his cousin was narcing for the enemy. And Legend might have even told them about her. It was hard for her to believe that he would betray her, but why wouldn't he if he would betray his own cousin? But what she couldn't figure out is why Legend hadn't told John-Boy and his crew that she was hiding out at the Camden house, too? Didn't he know?

Noticing she was in a particularly bad neighborhood, Chastity slowed down, and started

173

looking around for a good location to do what she had to do. Spotting a littered abandoned lot, she pulled over. There was a rusty trash can next to the lot, even better, she thought. She got out her car and popped her trunk, pulling out a plastic bag inside, along with a can of gasoline she'd purchased with some of the cash Hunter had given her. Looking around to make sure there was no one around, she put the bag in the can, poured some of the gasoline inside, then struck a match and threw it inside. She then quickly got in the car and drove off.

Her bloody clothes and her vomit now burning, it was time to figure out what to do next. She had to get to Hunter and let him know he was in more danger than he knew. As she got on the New Jersey Turnpike she knew she was taking a chance heading for his house in Long Island, but it was the only place she knew to look for him.

Once she got to Long Island, she circled his block three times, trying to see if anything looked suspicious, but finally decided to park and go inside. Once inside she saw the place had been ransacked. Pictures were torn from the wall, drapes pulled from the window, furniture was turned over, and the contents of cabinet drawers were spilled out onto the floor. Even the medicine cabinet in the bathroom had been pulled loose. Whoever was inside was definitely looking for something. The security alarm had been disarmed, which meant to Chastity that Legend was involved, since as far as she knew, Legend and her were only the ones who knew the code besides Hunter. "I still can't believe that nigga would do this shit," she said out loud as she made her way to the bedroom.

The one thing she hadn't found was the one thing she was hoping she wouldn't; Hunter's dead body.

That might mean there was a still chance he was alive, though she'd begun to doubt it after every call she'd made trying to contact him went unanswered.

The bedroom was in the same state as the rest of the house, in fact worse. The bed mattress had been torn to shreds, all of the clothes from the walk-in closet were strewn across the room, and it even looked like someone had taken a crowbar to the walls, revealing the wooden slats behind the plaster. But her mouth dropped open when she saw that the air conditioner, though severely dented was still intact. She quickly dropped to her knees and opened it. *Yes! It's still there!* Her breath quickened as she started stuffing stacks of money into her shoulder bag, then found some canvas and leather duffle bags and started stuffing those, too. It was hard to believe that Hunter had trusted her with his hiding place when he hadn't even told Legend about it, but thank God he did, she thought.

She pulled out her telephone and dialed Jackie's number again. "Yo, girl, I need you. Hurry up and gimme a call. This is some emergency shit," she said urgently into the voice mail system.

She started hauling the duffle bags downstairs to put them in the trunk of her car when she noticed a Federal Express package partially hidden under a downed drape and another one by r a toppled over chair. She picked them up and threw them into her shoulder bag, and continued onto her car. It took six trips for her to get all the bags in the vehicle. On the last trip she gathered up some of her clothes she found strewn on the floor, and as an afterthought grabbed the gun from the safe before locking it back up.

She climbed in the front seat of the car, and contemplated her next move.

Shay

She had to find some way to let Hunter know what was going on, and not to trust John-Boy, Danny or Legend. She reached into her shoulder bag for her cell phone to try and contact Hunter one more time. As she pulled out the phone, the Federal Express packages came into view. Curious, she picked one up and opened it. Inside was a cheap cell phone, identical to the one she'd accused of Hunter as using as his ho phone. *What the hell?* She turned it over twice, studying it before switching it on. She hit the menu button and then the contacts, and to her surprise there was one number programmed inside. *I wonder if . . . no . . . but maybe . . .* She took a deep breath and hit the call button. Even if it was some ho, she might know where Hunter was. Then she'd deal with him later about being in touch with some other bitch.

She almost dropped the telephone when she heard an unfamiliar male voice answer, "You okay?"

"Who's this?" she said when she regained her composure.

There was silence on the other line for a moment, then came back the reply. "Who is this?"

"I asked first."

"This is a friend of Hunter's."

"Well," Chastity said, her mind racing. "This is another friend of Hunter's."

"Shall I play a guessing game as to whom?" the man asked.

"Do you know where Hunter is?" Chastity asked, ignoring his question.

"Is this Chastity?"

"Who is this?" Chastity asked, shocked that whoever it was knew her name.

176

"Like I said, this is a friend of Hunter's. Where did you get this phone?"

Chastity shifted in her seat, and she wondered how to answer. "It doesn't matter," she finally said. "I got it, and that's it. Now, do you know where Hunter is?"

"Do you?"

"Look, I don't have time to be playing no fucking games!" Chastity screamed into the phone. "If you know where he is let him know I gotta talk to him! If you don't know, stop wasting my fucking –"

"Chastity, don't hang up!" the voice said urgently. "Where are you located right now?"

"Fuck you, motherfucker," Chastity screamed. "I don't know you, bitch."

"Please, try and calm down," the man's voice took on a soothing tone. "I know you don't know me, but I know you. Or at least I know of you. I know your full name is Chastity Eileen Jones. I know you live on Fifth Avenue. I know your father is Ronald Jones, and he's locked up at Woodbourne State Correctional Facility. I know that –"

"How do you know so much about me? Who is this?" Chastity said frantically.

"I'll say it again," the man said. "I'm a friend of Hunter's. And I know that you must have been, or still are at his house because that's the only way you could have gotten this phone."

"Yeah? Did you know that someone else was there? That someone tore his shit up looking for something?"

There was a pause. "No," the man said. "That I didn't know, but it doesn't surprise me. But why were

you there? Why aren't you at the safe house in Camden?"

"Because . . . because six guys came in looking for Hunter, and they shot every thing up." Chastity couldn't hold back her tears any longer. "Because Hulk and Rhino were tortured and killed, and the only way I escaped was by hiding in the bath tub."

"Shit."

"Yeah, shit," Chastity said. "And I have to find Hunter, because I have to let him know –" she hesitated, still not knowing how much to trust this unknown voice. ". . . because I have to let him know some things."

"Where are you now?" the man asked.

"Where are you? And what's your name?" she asked in return.

"Okay, Chastity. My name is Bill, and I'm in Manhattan. In midtown. Now where are you?"

"Do you know where Hunter is?"

"No. I'm trying to find him just like you. He should have picked up his package . . . picked up the phone you're using . . . a couple of hours ago, but it sounds like it might have been a good thing he didn't since you say someone was there."

"How do you know, Hunter?"

'Chastity, we don't have time for this –"

"How do you know him?" she persisted.

"I've known him since he moved here from California. Okay?" Bill said with exasperation evident in his voice. "We're good friends, and you can trust me."

Chastity shook her head. "I don't know who I can trust."

"I can understand that, and I understand why. But I'm telling you that you can trust me." There was a pause. "Hell, you know the information that your

178

attorney, Gephardt, has been getting? I've been the one supplying him, okay? So . . . think you can trust me now?"

Chastity breathed in sharply. "How do you. . .? I mean . . . can we meet up?"

"Where are you?"

"I'm in Long Island. In my car. In front of Hunter's house."

"Why are you still there?"

"I haven't decided where to go next," Chastity answered. "I guess we should meet up?"

"No. Just in case one of us is being tailed, we don't need to have both of us pinched," Bill said. "But we keep in contact, using this phone, and this phone only. It's clean, and can't be traced. Got that?"

"Got it," Chastity nodded. "But wait, what about this other package. It's too thin to have a cell phone in it. You sent something else?"

"What other package?"

"There were two Federal Express packages at Hunter's house," Chastity explained, withdrawing the other package from her bag as she drove.

"I only sent one. Open it up," Bill said.

She pulled over and tore open the package. Inside was a DVD, marked "For Your Viewing Pleasure."

"Is there somewhere you can go to see what's on the DVD?" Bill said when she told him the contents of the package.

She thought about it for a moment. She could go back to her place, but she'd already taken enough of a chance going to Hunter's house, there was no sense in pushing her luck. She could head to Jackie's place, though. She didn't know why her friend wasn't

answering her telephone, but she had Jackie's keys, just like Jackie had hers. "Yeah, I'll call you as soon as I look at it," she told Bill.

"Jackie?" Chastity called out as she entered the girl's apartment. She didn't expect an answer, and she got none. She walked into the living room, then strode into the kitchen, bedroom, and bathroom, looking for some clue as to Jackie's whereabouts. Maybe she got one of the Jerry's to take her out of town, Chastity thought. But why wouldn't she be picking up her phone?

She went back into the living room and turned on Jackie's television, then popped the DVD inside. Just as the picture began to emerge, the bootleg cell phone rang.

"Yeah?"

"It's me. Bill."

"Good timing." Chastity sat down on the couch. "I'm getting ready to watch it now."

"Okay. Turn up the volume as loud as it gets so I can at least hear."

She used the remote to turn up the sound as the DVD began to play, then dropped it in horror at the video started playing in front of her.

There was a barely recognizable Jackie, naked, her face badly bruised and swollen, on her knees in front of a man whose pants were dropped down at his ankles. Next to her stood another man, pressing a gun against her head, saying, "You bite my man's dick, and I'ma blow your fuckin' brains out, bitch." Jackie was crying as she opened her mouth, and took the man inside, and

180

RAW

started bobbing her up and down while tears streamed down her face and sobs wracked her body. The man getting his dick sucked grabbed her by the hair and shoved her all the way down, causing her to gag and cough as she tried to come up for air.

The man holding the gun started laughing, and looked directly into the camera and said, "See that, Hunt? Your bitch don't even know how to give head. I guess we'se gonna haveta find something else she might be better at." He turned back to Jackie. "Stand up, bitch." He slapped her upside the head with the gun, obviously deeming she was moving to slow. "Do what the fuck I said." Jackie struggled to her feet, and the man who had spoken into the camera, motioned for the other man to get on the bed. He grinned as he complied, sitting down on the edge of the bed, then lying down so that his legs were still on the floor.

"Let's see how good the bitch is at doing it cowgirl style."

Jackie continued to sob as she was made to straddle the man, and move her body on top of him as he grabbed her hips and braced his feet on the floor so he could thrust hard into her. The other man, walked over, took out his dick and began stroking it as he talked into the camera. "Well, Hunter, nigga, look like your bitch know how to ride that horse, huh? Giddie the fuck up, bitch. She any good, Ricky?"

"Yeah," Ricky answered. "Bitch got some good ass pussy."

The man with the gun slapped Jackie on the ass hard. "Move that ass. I said move that ass." He looked at the camera again, and then grinned and winked. "She sure got a mighty fine fuckin' ass, Hunt, man," he said. "Fuckin' irresistible." He then turned from the camera,

and still holding the gun with one hand, he used his other to guide his dick to the crack of Jackie's ass. When she jumped and let out a little yelp he pressed the gun against her head, and said, "You fuckin' do what I say or youse a dead bitch. Now, reach your hands behind you and open up them ass cheeks. Do what I say!" Sobbing hysterically Jackie did what she was told while Ricky laughed.

"Now, raise up a little, but don't let my man's dick slip out, you hear?" The man with the gun said. He motioned to the guy holding the camera, who up to this point had been silent. "John-Boy, come here. Hold this," the man said, handing off the gun. "Keep it pointed at the bitch's head."

"Danny, man, how the fuck you want me to hold the gun and the camera, too?" John-Boy complained.

"Just do it," Danny commanded.

Danny then put one arm around Jackie's throat from behind, and bent a little at the knees. "Now, let's see how good you are at taking dick up the pussy and the ass, bitch." He gave a hard thrust, and Jackie screamed at the top of lungs and tried to get away.

"Oh yeah, this is a nice tight ass," Danny moaned. "Oh fuck, yeah. Come here, bitch. Take your new daddy's dick." He started pushing Jackie's body down on his dick while pushing himself further and further in, his eyes rolling upwards in ecstasy, ignoring her frantic screams and attempts to escape his grasp. When he was finally all the way inside her ass he let out a load groan of pleasure. "Shit, hold on a minute, I don't wanna cum yet. I wanna enjoy this ass."

"Yo, Danny, man. You fuckin' with my groove," Ricky said. "I can't move my dick in her like this."

182

Shay

"Now, tell your nigga how much you enjoyed fuckin' us, Chastity." John-Boy's voice demanded. "And tell him the next DVD he gets is gonna show me puttin' this gun up that pussy and blowin' your insides out."

"I told you, I'm not Chastity," Jackie said through her cracked and swollen lips. "My name is Jackie."

"Yeah? Well, why was you at Chastity's apartment? And why you say you was Chastity in the first place?"

"I was only playin'." Jackie started sobbing. "My name is Jackie Faison. For real. My name is Jackie."

"Yeah? Well, whatever the fuck your name is, you'd better hope that nigga Hunter feels sorry for your ass, because like I said, the next DVD he gets is gonna show you deaded out," John-Boy taunted. He then moved so that he was directly in front of the camera. "So, nigga. What you think? Jealous because we can fuck your bitch better than you?" He started laughing. "Yeah, nigga, you always tryin' to come off like you every bitch's champion, well, if you wanna save your own bitch, you know what you gotta do. As soon as you give us the shit we want, we let your bitch go and ya'll muthafuckas can go ridin' off into the night as far as I care. So man up, and do what you gotta do, nigga." The camera then clicked off, and the television went sky blue.

"Chastity! Chastity! Pick up the damn phone!"

She looked down the on the floor, not even realizing she had dropped the phone. "Bill, we gotta find Hunter," she said, sobbing hysterically. "We gotta let him know they got Jackie. They said they're going to kill her. She's my best friend. Oh God!" She dropped the

184

phone down again, and started rocking herself back and forth on the couch, her arms folded over her chest as if she were trying to give herself a comforting hug.

"Chastity, try to calm down. I need you to be calm," she heard Bill shouting into the telephone. She picked it up again, but it was a few moments before she could speak.

"What do we do now?" she said finally. "How do we get in touch with Hunter, and what it is they want from him?"

"I don't know," Bill said. "But I need you to play that DVD again and –"

"NO!" Chastity shouted.

"Shh, listen. You're right. Where are you? I'll come and pick it up. I need to look at it to see if I can find any clues as to where they might be holding your friend."

Chapter Twelve

Bill had said that he would be there in an hour, and Chastity used the time to take a short hot shower, then dress in some of the clothes she had stored at Jackie's apartment, grateful that she wouldn't have to go down and retrieve any clothes from the trunk of her car. Besides, the clothes she had at Jackie's were fancier, and she knew she'd have to look good to pull off the moves she'd decided to make to save her friend and her man.

With twenty-five minutes before Bill's expected arrival, Chastity sat down in front of the computer and Jackie's bedroom and turned it on, in order to make a copy of the DVD so that both she and Bill would have a copy. She fought back tears as Jackie's screen saver appeared – it was a picture of Chastity and Jackie as preteens, laughing and holding ice cream cones as they stood in front of an open fire hydrant in happier times.

"No crying, no crying," Chastity chanted to herself. "It's time to plan. Time to make things happen. And there ain't no bitch who has better moves than me."

Despite what she'd told Bill, she forced herself to play the seven-minute DVD two more times, looking for clues herself. But she still had no idea where John-Boy and his crew were holding Jackie. And she still couldn't figure out exactly how Legend fit into the equation. She knew he was involved somehow, because Rhino had said John-Boy had been talking to him on the

telephone, and no one else would have had Hunter's security alarm code.

But Legend would have been able to confirm that they'd picked up the wrong woman. Maybe he'd had a change of heart and let them think Jackie was her so that they would torture the wrong woman? She shivered at the thought. Jackie wasn't Legend's favorite person, but they did develop a good relationship over the years. She couldn't see him allowing them to hurt Jackie like that. Or maybe he didn't know they'd gotten Jackie. But how else could they have gotten her address? They had to get it from Legend. It was obvious they didn't know her, or they would have known what she looked like. No, they had to get the information from Legend.

She popped the two DVD's out of the computer and placed one in her bag and waited for Bill to arrive. She didn't have to wait long.

"Who is it?" she demanded when the front door bell rang.

"Me," came back the now familiar voice.

"Prove it," she demanded.

"It's me, Bill," the voice said impatiently.

"Call me on the phone."

She opened the door as the cell phone in her hand began to ring, and a short dark-skinned clean-cut man wearing a light gray suit with a white shirt and red tie quickly walked in. She shut the door behind him.

"Do you have the DVD?" he said abruptly, cutting right to the chase.

"I want some questions answered first," Chastity said coldly. "Have a seat."

"I don't have time —"

"Make the time," Chastity commanded.

Shay

Bill frowned, then walked over to the sofa and sat down, though one of his legs started bouncing up and down, showing his impatience and displeasure. "What do you want to know?" he asked.

"How do you know Hunter?" she said, seating herself on the loveseat across from him.

"We occasionally work together," Bill said grimly.

"Work together on what?" Chastity crossed her legs.

"On business," he snapped.

Chastity shook her head. "Uh uh. Come better than that."

Bill leaned back on the couch. "I assume you know what kind of business Hunter is in. Am I right? Well, make your assumptions from there."

"Are you his connection?" Chastity pressed on.

Bill hesitated. "Let's just say I'm one of the people who make the connections happen."

"Oh? Care to explain?"

"No," Bill said firmly.

"Okay, then," Chastity said, "When's the last time you've seen Hunter, and where was he?"

Bill snorted. "I haven't actually seen Hunter in a couple of years –"

"What?"

"—but we talk every couple of days," Bill continued, "using cell phones that I send him. I spoke to him three days ago, on Tuesday, and I was supposed to be speak to him this afternoon, but he never picked up the phone. Which as I told you earlier, I had delivered to his house this morning. Only when I called there was no answer. Then when I got your call I thought it was him."

"Where was he when you last spoke to him?"

188

"In Harlem, at his cousin's house." Bill crossed his arms. "You do realize that every minute we waste here is another minute your friend is being tortured, right? You okay with that?"

"Are you?"

"What's that supposed to mean?"

Chastity leaned forward. "I've been in the game a minute, and I know how it's played. Niggas think bitches are dispensable. You don't think I know that shit? So you want the DVD for clues as to John-Boy's location, huh? Well, do you want to know it to save Jackie, or do you want to know it so you can take your time and plot on how to get to John-Boy? Answer me that, bitch."

"Does it make a difference?"

"Fuck yeah, it does," Chastity snapped. "I want to know if you're gonna waste time plotting to get at John-Boy and this Wheatie nigga or if you're gonna try and rescue my friend before they kill her. That shit makes a helluva lot of difference to me."

Bill's eyes narrowed as he looked at her. "You know how Hunter's parents died?"

Chastity nodded her head, remembering what he'd told about her father's drive-by shooting and his mother's heart attack because of it. "Yeah. And?"

"You asked me how I met Hunter. Well . . . " Bill hesitated. "Well, he and I were both working for a nigga named Jeezy, back in the day."

"Hunter told me about him."

Bill ignored the interruption. "Jeezy found out that there was a narc in his organization, and a little later he found out it was me —"

Chastity gasped as Bill continued.

189

"He sent folks after me, but my people moved me underground. They were supposed to move my wife and son underground, too, but Jeezy's people got to them first. Hunter and Legend walked in the Jeezy's house just as they were stripping my wife, my pregnant wife, and preparing to rape her. He told them to let her go, but when they refused he and Legend blew everyone in the house away, and then set my wife free. My son," Bill's voice cracked, "it was too late for my son. They'd already killed him. He was only six-years-old."

"Oh my God," Chastity said softly.

Bill took a deep breath. "My wife suffered a nervous break-down, and miscarried a few days later. My . . . my people tried to keep what happened from me at first, but when I found out I rubbed out everybody in Jeezy's organization that Hunter hadn't. Then I went looking for Hunter and Legend. Not to kill them, but to thank them. I've been looking out for them ever since."

"What happened to your wife?"

"It took awhile, but she's okay now. We just had a little girl a few months ago." Bill smiled. "We named her Diana, after the Greek goddess. You know, the hunter."

"I'm happy for you, but, well," Chastity paused. "I don't understand, something. You asked me if I knew how Hunter's parents were killed. I don't get the connection."

Bill pulled his head back, as if surprised. "Well," he said slowly, "how did he say they were killed?"

Chastity recounted Hunter's story, but Bill shook his head the whole time she was talking. When she finished, Bill said, "He lied."

"What do you mean?"

190

"Hunter's mother was there when his father was caught in the drive-by. When some of the gang members found out that she was planning to testify against them, they broke into her house. They raped and pistol-whipped her right there in front of Hunter, while one of the guys held him down and made him watch, just for laughs."

"The fuck –" Chastity's mouth continued to move, but she couldn't form any words.

"After they finished, they shot her. In cold blood. Then they shot at Hunter, and must have thought they killed him, but actually he fainted." Bill paused. "It was understandable. He was only ten, you know. But Hunter has blamed himself for her death ever since. He never told the police who it was who killed his mother, but when he was sixteen he bought a gun and went after them himself. Legend was only fifteen, but he helped him dispose of the bodies."

"I . . . I had no idea," Chastity stammered.

"Well, you should know what kind of man you're dealing with. He's a stand-up nigga if there ever was one. Do you remember, a few years back, them talking on the news about a Haitian woman who was raped by some gang members in a D.C. housing project? They even made her give her 16-year-old son a blow-job."

"Yeah, I think I remember hearing about that sick shit."

"Well, when Hunter heard, he made a trip down to D. C. He didn't know the woman, and he didn't know the people who did it, but he found out who they were and killed all of them," Bill let out a sad chuckle. "If I'd known he was making the trip I woulda went with him."

191

Shay

Chastity sat in silence for a few minutes, letting what Bill had told her sink in.

"So, you still wanna ask me if we're going to try and save your friend?" Bill leaned back and crossed his arms again.

Chastity lowered her eyes. "I'm sorry. I shouldn't have come at you like that. So what's the next move?"

"Give me the DVD. Let me take it down to the lab and have some of my people go over it. We can enhance the picture, zoom in on little details, see what can be found," Bill said. "And meanwhile, we'll have to hope that Hunter or Legend contacts one of us."

"Bill, Legend is working for that Wheatie nigga."

"What?" Bill's mouth fell open. "Why do you say that?"

Chastity shared everything that had went down at the Camden house, including Rhino's last words, and how when she went to the Hunter's Long Island mansion, the security alarm had been disarmed.

"No, no, I still can't believe it," Bill said shaking his head. "I've never seen two cousins as close and Hunter and Legend. Legend would never just turn on him for no reason. It just wouldn't make sense."

Chastity almost blurted out her suspicions as to why Legend betrayed Hunter, but caught herself. If neither Hunter nor Legend had told Bill about the fight over her, they obviously didn't want him to know. And anyway, she reasoned, if she did tell Bill he might just think she had an overblown ego to think she could be the reason for the betrayal. So instead, she said, "Well, you never know what a person is capable of doing until they do it. So if Legend does get in touch with you, watch

192

what you say. And if Hunter gets in touch with you, let him know the deal." She reached into her bag and handed Bill a copy of the DVD. "If you find anything useful, promise to let me know?"

Bill stood up, slipping the DVD into his jacket pocket. "I don't want you to make any stupid moves, Chastity, so I'm not going to promise you anything except that I'm on it. You need to get to somewhere safe and stay put. And I don't want you staying here, just in case Jackie convinces them to come here and check for themselves that she lives here and not at your apartment. Do you have somewhere else to go?"

"I could go to Jackie's mom's house." She gave him the address, choosing not to argue with him her not being involved. She knew it was pointless. The man's mind was already made up.

She didn't know where she was going to go, but she knew where she wasn't, and that was to Jackie's mom's house. There was no way she was going to sit in her mother's face knowing what she knew about what was going on with Jackie. She drove up Fifth Avenue, then stopped the car at 93rd Street, across from Central Park, then pulled the DVD out of her bag and popped it into the car's DVD player and forced herself to watch it again. She muted the volume, and concentrated on the background view. After her fourth viewing she noticed it. A poster on the wall, announcing a listening party for an up and coming hip-hop artist. She'd seen the poster before, Raheem had one in his apartment because the guy's producer had bought one of his beats for the CD.

193

But it was the only place she'd seen the poster. The artist didn't have enough money to pay for a street team to distribute them throughout the city, and she'd heard Raheem moaning and groaning that because of that the listening party was going to be a dud. So if the poster was up on the wall, it might mean that one of the people in the apartment knew the artist. Her heart started beating rapidly. And it might mean that they'd be at the party. She reached in her bag for the cell phone to call Bill. Shit, I musta left it at the apartment. She drove back to Jackie's building on West 63rd Street, and was about to park the car when she noticed two strange men standing in front of the apartment house, wearing sunglasses, their arms folded over their chests. She held her breath, praying that they hadn't noticed her, as she continued up the street. Maybe it was just a coincidence two men standing there, after all, there was really nothing suspicious about them. But she didn't want to take any chance. She went back to the same spot she'd left on 93rd Street. Pulling out her own cell phone she tried Hunter's number one more time, but again she only reached his voice mail. She started to slip her phone back into her bag, when an idea hit her. She quickly tapped in a number on the cell.

"Speak."

"Raheem, baby. What you into tonight?" Chastity purred into the phone.

"Chas? Girl, where da fuck you been? Shit, a nigga been thirstin' for some of that good pussy. When you gonna let me tap that shit again?"

Chastity rolled her eyes, but kept the sexy tone in her voice. "And I've been thirsting for my daddy's dick. You home? I'm on my way over."

194

"Naw, B., I'm at the studio, layin' down some tracks. I probably won't be rollin' outta here until about four in the morning."

"Which studio are you at, Rah? Let me come over."

"Shit, baby, uh, I, uh, would love to see your fine ass, but this might not be a good time," his voice lowered. "You know, I'm busy and shit."

Yeah, nigga. What you mean is you got some ho sitting on a stool making bitch eyes at you while you pushing them control levers. "Aw, daddy. I guess I'm going to have to put some ice cubes in this pussy because I'm hot as shit for you right about now."

"Damn, girl. You makin' a nigga's dick all hard and shit. Listen, why on't you roll in here in about two hours? I might be able to take a quick break and let's see if we can make it do what it do?"

"Word." Chastity didn't try to hide her excitement. "Give me the address." She grabbed a pen and paper and wrote down the address then quickly hung up. "Fuck two hours," she said to herself as she pulled down the vanity mirror in the car and fluffed up her hair and applied another coat of lip gloss. "A bitch gotta do what a bitch gotta do."

Twenty minutes later, she strode into the studio, head high and shoulders erect, and went straight for Raheem, ignoring the trio of cheap looking groupie types sitting behind him, and eyeing her like she was public enemy number one.

"Yo, Chas? What you doin' over here?" Raheem said, standing up quickly.

"Couldn't wait," she said, kissing him on the mouth while giving his dick a squeeze and licking her lips. She then turned to the girls as if noticing them for

195

the first time. "Oh, I didn't realize you had company. You were that hard up waiting on me?"

"Fuck you, bitch," one of the girls snarled.

Chastity snorted then turned back to Raheem. "You want me to get rid of these tricks for you, daddy?"

"Bitch, I will kick your fucking ass," the girl said standing up, her hands flailing at her side.

Chastity chuckled, then walked over to the coat rack and put the strap of her shoulder bag on a hanger. Then she leisurely strolled back over to where the girls sat, removing her earrings as she did so.

Raheem moved in front of her, as if making a half-hearted attempt to stop any fight, but he didn't try to push her back. Chastity hid her smile as she noticed the pride in his eyes as one of the other men in the studio shouted, "Yo, Raheem, you got bitches fighting ova you, nigga?" followed by a chorus of laughter.

"Naw, naw, ain't gonna be no fightin' up in this joint," Raheem said, though he still didn't put a hand out to stop Chastity's progress.

"Now, what were you saying about kicking my ass, little girl?" she said when she was standing in front of the girl. "Bring it, bitch." Chastity balled up her fists, her adrenaline racing, hoping that the girl would make a move on her. All of the frustrations of the past ten or twelve hours were making her nerves tingle, and made her eager to have someone to unleash her anger on. But something in her voice must have warned the girl she was in danger of being beaten senseless, because she suddenly backed down, turning around and returning to her stool with her friends.

"Yeah, that's what I thought," Chastity taunted. She turned to Raheem. "Why don't you call me when you get rid of these skank bitches and you're ready for a

real woman." She walked over to him and gave his dick another squeeze. "One that knows how to handle a real nigga like you, big daddy."

Raheem grinned ear-to-ear as she licked his neck. "Sheet, I'm ready to roll outta here right, now, Chas."

"Aw, naw the hell you ain't, nigga. We only got two more tracks to go," one of the men in the studio said. "Get your shit off later."

"Handle your business, Rah." Chastity gave him a peck on the lips. "I'll see you next week some time."

"A fuckin' week? Hell naw, Chas," Raheem protested. "Here. Take some money and go shoppin' or something. Meet me back up here in like an hour so we can do our thang." He pulled out his platinum money clip and peeled off ten one-hundred bills and placed them in Chastity's outstretched hands. She looked at the money and then back up at Raheem with a raised eyebrow. "And?"

"The fuck you mean, with that 'and' shit?" Raheem said loudly, though the twinkle in his eyes let her know he enjoyed the show they were performing.

She looked down at her hand again and tapped her foot. "And?" she repeated.

Raheem laughed. "Girl, you ain't shit." He peeled twenty more one-hundred dollar bills. "Now make sure you bring your pretty ass back ova here to a nigga in an hour. I mean it."

"I'll be here, daddy." She turned to the girls and smirked. "Now see? That's how a real bitch rolls." She balled up one of the hundred dollar bills that Raheem had given her and threw at the girls' feet. "Here's some bus fare. Your asses best not be here when I get back."

Shay

The girls glared at her but said nothing as she sashayed over to the coat rack and reached for her bag, using her body to block the view as she quickly dipped into Raheem's jacket pocket and pulled out his keys. She blew Raheem an air kiss and walked out the door.

Chapter Thirteen

The men who'd she been with who were real gangsta never had their guns on display, but the wannabes like Raheem like so many in the hip-hop world always wanted to show off their irons. She thought she'd watched him enough times showing off as he played with gun collection to know how to put on a silencer, but it wasn't as easy as she thought. And to her dismay, she couldn't find one that fit the .45 glock she'd gotten from Hunter's safe. Luckily, she did find one that matched a .38 automatic she found in the gun cabinet. Making sure the clip was full, and the safety on, she slipped it into her bag, then opened up the drawer in cabinet to see what else she could find. She picked out two stun guns, a Taser, handcuffs, a can of mace, and a stiletto knife. She then locked the cabinet back up and headed downstairs.

"Jorge, let me talk to you out here for a moment," she said smiling at the doorman as he opened the door for her.

"Of course, Miss Jones," he said, grinning, obviously anticipating the fifty dollars she usually pressed into his palm after a visit with Raheem.

"Listen," she said, sidling up close to him when they were on the sidewalk in front of the building. "I wasn't here." She placed some bills in his palm, then closed his fingers around it.

"But Miss Jones –"

Shay

"I wasn't here," she repeated, smiling at him.

"Miss Jones, I hope you didn't –"

"No, no, no, Jorge. Open your hand and look down." She smiled as his eyes widened when he saw the ten one-hundred dollar bills. "I couldn't have done anything, Jorge, because I wasn't here, right?" She gave him two light pats on the cheek.

"I certainly didn't see you, Miss Jones," Jorge said with a grin. "You need a taxi?"

"No, I'm fine," she said over her shoulder. "See you later."

Thank God she'd always treated Jorge right, and thank God Raheem always treated him like shit, she thought as she crossed the street and got into her car and pulled off. Legend had taught her well, treat the little people well because you never know when you'll need them.

It was eleven o'clock when she pulled into the parking lot of the club holding the listening party. The poster had said ten, but she knew that there would be few people before midnight. That would give her time to scope out the place, and figure out her best plan of action. She pulled out her phone again and called Hunter, hoping against hope that he'd answer, but again she only reached his voice mail.

As she expected the club was almost empty. She looked around, letting her eyes adjust to the darkness as she tried to find the best location to see everyone who came through the door, when she spotted him. Danny. The ass man. She tried to calm her breathing as she watched him, bopping his head to the music blaring from the six-foot Dolby speakers. He was standing next to one of the club bouncers, occasionally cupping his hand over his mouth and leaning into the guy's ear to say

200

something. She sat there sizing him up. A low-life nigga with some paper, but the type who would be intimidated by someone with too much class. She'd have to be ghetto bitch to really get his attention.

She ordered a glass of champagne, then walked over. She jiggled her glass provocatively, then placed it against her ample cleavage, glancing at the bouncer's name tag. "You're Tony, huh?"

"Yeah, why?"

"Raheem said I should ask for you so I can get into the VIP section." She answered.

"Raheem who?"

She gave an exaggerated roll of the eyes. "Raheem Raheem, man, come on nigga. Why you fuckin' trying to quiz me?" She turned to Danny and flashed him a smile. "You believe this shit?" she said as if they were in on some conspiracy together. She looked back at the bouncer. "Raheem as in Raheem Martin. My big brother. The nigga's who wrote the beat they rockin' right now."

"Yeah?" the bouncer challenged her. "Well, where the nigga at now?"

"He's at the studio, layin' down some tracks. What? You want me to call him right now and put you on blast?" She pulled out her iPhone and pushed a button and flashed it in front of the bouncer's nose so that he could see it was indeed Raheem's name and picture popping up on the screen. Then she pulled the cell back to her ear, using her thumb to hit the off button as she did so.

"Yo, Raheem," she said into the dead line. "I'm at the club and this muthafucka givin' me some shit about getting' in VIP. Say he don't even know you."

Shay

"I ain't say all that," the bouncer said quickly. "I was just –"

"Yeah, nigga," Chastity sucked her teeth. "I know what you was 'just.' Raheem, you wanna talk to this nigga or what? Cause I was gonna just lay here and wait for you, but I'm not sitting up on here no fuckin' bar stool all night. Hold on." She pulled the phone from her ear and placed it against her chest as she addressed the bouncer. "My brother said for you to get to hoppin' or for me to get the manager," she said with a sneer. "Your choice."

"Yo, ma, I ain't say I wasn't puttin' you in VIP," the bouncer said hurriedly. "Just follow me."

"Yeah, that's right, nigga." Chastity let out a chuckle. "See what a bitch gotta go through to get her props?" She narrowed her eyes as she gave Danny a slow up and down look. "Damn, nigga. You lookin' fine. Ain't I see you at Raheem's New Year Party, man?"

"Uh, you mighta seen me," Danny gave a little laugh. "There was so many muthafuckas up in that joint ain't no tellin' who saw who."

"You got that shit right." Chastity tapped him lightly on the chest. *Full of shit, nigga. Raheem wasn't even in town on New Year's Eve.* "What's your name again?"

"Danny."

"Well, Danny, why don't you come over to the table and keep a bitch company. Raheem won't be here for a couple of hours. A bitch gets lonely and shit."

"You wearin' them pants, ma," Danny said as he followed behind her. "You got one tight ass."

"Like it?" Chastity gave a little wiggle before sitting down. "You don't even know the half of it."

"Whatchoo mean?"

202

"Never mind," Chastity chucked him under the chin. "Maybe we'll talk about that shit later. Right now I wanna know about you. What's your story?"

"Naw, let's talk about you! You really Raheem's little sister?" Danny leaned forward excitedly. "Man, your bro be layin' down some tight-ass beats."

He went on for another thirty minutes dropping names, and laying down game. It turned out that just like Raheem was a real-life producer and a wannabe gangsta, Danny was a real-life gangsta and a wannabe producer.

"Look, Raheem's in the studio now with some new guy who's tryinta come up, but he got some time scheduled with Lil Mama, tomorrow night. Why don't you stop through?"

Danny eyes widened. "Yeah? That would be the shit, but word, I don't really know your brother like that, ma."

"Well, I do. And I'm bettin' we can work something out," Chastity looked down at his groin area suggestively.

"Heh," Danny grinned and moved his chair closer to hers. "I bet we can. Whatchoo got in mind, girl?"

"Damn, nigga. A bitch don't wanna put her shit all outh there."

"Come on, girl. You talking to Danny now. Speak your mind."

"Tell me what you workin' with." Chastity said, putting her hand on his thigh.

"Check it out for yourself." Danny took her hand and moved it over his crotch.

Chastity gave it a squeeze, and then let out a little moan. "Oh yeah, nigga. That's what's up. I bet you can work that shit, too."

Shay

"I ain't never had no bitch complain."

"Yeah, well," Chastity gave his dick another squeeze. "I like it rough. You think you can handle that?"

Danny started breathing hard and Chastity felt his dick harden in his pants. "Yeah, I got you, ma."

"Word? Cause I like it real rough. I wanna nigga who can put a hurtin' on a bitch." Chastity rubbing Danny's crotch. "And . . ."

"Yeah? And?" Danny said expectantly.

"I don't want you putting my shit on blast, okay? Can I trust you?" Chastity grabbed the complimentary bottle of Moet the club manager had sent over and poured herself a glass.

"Yeah, you know this shit is just between me and you, ma." Danny said impatiently, squirming in his seat, and placing Chastity's hand back on his groin.

"Well, I like it . . . well . . . you ever . . . you know . . ." Chastity leaned forward and whispered in Danny's ear. "I like it when a nigga puts a big black dick up my tight ass. Can you handle that?" She gave his ear a lick.

"Fuck yeah," Danny groaned. "I been thinking about tappin' that ass since you walked in wearing them spandex, girl."

"Word?" You gonna make a bitch cream right here, talkin' like that." Chastity started breathing hard in Danny's ear. "Shit, nigga. How far you live from here? Let's go do this thing. We got another hour before Raheem gets here. Just give me a taste so I can see how you lay it down."

"There's a hotel right around the corner," Danny croaked. "We can walk there in five minutes."

work." Chastity grabbed her bag off the table. "That'll

"Let me see that dick," Chastity said as soon as they entered the motel room. She grabbed him around the neck and gave him a tight squeeze, grinding her pelvic into his. "I want to deep-throat that shit, and have you cum in my mouth. Then I want to suck you hard again and have you fuck my ass until I bleed."

"Shit, you come at a nigga hard, don't you? I like that shit," Danny said, pushing her slightly away as he unbuckled his pants. "Damn, ma. You know what? I don't even know your fuckin' name."

Chastity giggled. "You wanna my name?"

"Yeah." Danny dropped his pants to the floor.

"My name . . . is . . . Chastity . . . Jones . . . and I heard you were looking for me, bitch." With that she took the Taser she'd concealed in her hand and placed it against his neck, turning it on full blast.

His mouth dropped opened, and his eyes looked like they were going to bulge out of their sockets as he started hopping up and down as the Taser buzzed and crackled. "Aaagh . . . " he screamed.

She waited for him to fall unconscious, but he just stood there hopping, screaming, and looking like he was having an epileptic fit. Frustrated, she moved the Taser from his neck to his groin, and pressed it against his scrotum, giving it another full blast. It took another ten seconds, but he finally fell to his knees, though he still maintained consciousness. While he lay writhing on the floor, she reached inside her bag for the stun gun,

and shot once in the chest. His eyes finally rolled up in his eyes, and he was out.

She quickly handcuffed his hands behind his back and dragged him over to a chair. Taking duct tape and rope she'd purchased from a drug store earlier, she gagged him and tied him down then took off his shoes and socks. Then she sat on the bed, out of breath. *This shit sure looks easier on T.V.*

She waited for him to gain consciousness, then finally growing impatient she got the ice canister, filled it with water from the bathroom and dumped it over his head. He blinked his eyes a few times, then shook his head. Then when he looked up and saw her sitting in front of him with a gun pointed at his groin, he tried to let out a scream but the duct tape over his mouth stifled the sound.

"Okay, we're going to go through this pretty fast, I hope," Chastity said in a calm voice. "First I need to let you know I'm serious. So . . . " She paused, and took a deep breath, then aimed and fired. A bloody hole opened up in his ankle. "Shit, I was aiming for your big toe. Sorry about that. I think the silencer threw me off."

Danny's head was thrown back, and she could see he was trying to holler at the top of his lungs. She bit her lip, as the reality of what she was doing sunk it. She'd never shot anyone before, and never thought she'd have to. But, hell, it was either this nigger or Jackie, she thought. The memory of the video, and what Danny had put through Jackie through hardened her enough to continue.

"Calm down so we can talk," she said. She waited a few seconds. "I don't have much time. Either you calm down or I'm going to shoot again."

Danny started shaking his head furiously, his expression pleading with her to have some kind of pity. It might have worked if a picture of Jackie, battered and being brutally raped didn't flash in front of Chastity's eyes again.

"You calm yet?" she asked coldly.

Danny let out a muffled whimper, then nodded his head.

"Okay. You've got my friend, Jackie –"

Danny started shaking his head again.

Chastity sucked her teeth, then fired another shot. This time hitting the instep of Danny's foot. She let him go through a series of muffled yells again before saying, "Okay, we're going to try this again. You've got my friend, Jackie. Don't you?"

Tears streamed down Danny's face as he frantically nodded his head.

"Okay, then. And if I take off that tape you're going to tell me where she is?"

He nodded again.

She put down the gun, but picked up the stiletto knife lying next to her. She walked over to him and bent down. "Now, if I take this tape off and you start screaming, I'm going to slit your throat. And to show you I'm serious . . ." She took the knife and sliced a thin gash down his left cheek. She waited again for him to go through his writhing and muffled cries. "Finished?"

His head drooped, but he nodded.

"So, I'm going to loosen the tape, and you're going to tell me where the fuck you got my friend, right?"

He nodded again.

She slowly lifted the tape, but only halfway across his mouth. "Now, where is she?"

207

Shay

"Look, I don't know –"

Chastity slapped the tape back on him, and used the knife to slice off the lower portion of his left ear. "You feeling me now, motherfucker? Don't waste my time with no idle fucking conversation. I asked you a question. Or do I have to cut off your dick?"

Danny's body was wracked with unvoiced sobs; and tears, blood and snot covered his face as he frantically shook his head no.

"Now," Chastity pulled the tape off. "Where's Jackie?"

"In the Bronx. Tremont Avenue. 577 Tremont. Apartment 3F. Third Floor." Danny croaked, while breathing hard.

"Good. Is she still alive?"

"Yeah." Danny looked up at her with pleading eyes. "I ain't know she was your friend, ma. I wouldn'ta hurt if I did."

What a load of shit. "How many people are there with her?"

"Two, maybe three dudes."

"Okay. Where's your cell phone?"

"In my pants pocket."

Chastity quickly retrieved it. "Give me the number one of them niggas will pick up."

"What? I don't –"

Chastity gave him a warning look, then picked up the gun again. "Don't fuck with me, bitch."

"Okay, okay," Danny said quickly. He called off a number, and Chastity tapped it out on the phone. Before hitting the send button she put the phone down. "Now, here's how we're going to do this. I'm going to put this on speaker phone. And when your man picks up,

208

you're going to say you're going to be there in like an hour, and then ask who's there. Got it?"

Fresh tears started welling up in Danny's eyes, but he nodded.

Chastity kneeled down in front of him. "Listen, I don't know you and you don't know me. I don't have any bad feelings for you, I just want to get my girl and get outta town. Whatever shit there is between you and Hunter, fuck it, it's between you and Hunter. Me and Jackie don't care. You've got to promise me, that when this is all over you won't come after me or her. Okay?"

She could see hope spring into Danny's eyes as he obviously began to believe he was going to make it out the hotel room alive. "Yeah, ma. I ain't gonna have no hard feelings. I gotta respect for you takin' care of your shit and lookin' out for your girl."

"Good, because if you mess up this call, and one of those niggas get suspicious, then I'm not going to have a choice but dead you. Understand? And I don't wanna go to prison for no fucking murder, and I know you sure don't want to be deaded. We straight?"

"Yeah, I got this," Danny nodded, confidence beginning to creep into his voice. "Go ahead and call the nigga."

Chastity took a deep breath, then hit the send button.

It rang only twice before a man picked up. "Yeah?"

"John-Boy, what's goin' on? What y'all niggas doin'?" Danny said, nodding at Chastity as if to show he was following through on the agreement.

"Just chillin'. Why's what's up?"

"Nuttin', nigga. I just wanted to see what's up with you niggas. Who's over there?"

Shay

"Just me and Ricky. And this skank ho. Man, she's stanking up the joint. I'm bout to throw her in the fucking bathtub and turn on the hot water to get some of that smell outta this bitch. When we gonna do her?"

"Chill man," Danny yelled frantically. "Just leave her the fuck alone."

"What the fuck is wrong with you?" John-Boy said in a puzzled voice. "Why you trippin' all of the sudden?"

"Ain't nutthin' wrong with me, nigga. Just leave the girl alone until I get there, okay? Don't be fuckin' with her."

"Aight, B. Chill. It ain't all that serious. Youse the one said we was gonna –"

"Man," Danny shouted. "Fuck what I said, before. Leave the bitch alone until I get there. I'll be rolling through in about an hour."

"Yeah, well, whatever," John-Boy said. "Pick me up some Mickie D's. A nigga's got the munchies. This is one fucked up way to be spending my birthday."

Chastity hit the end button, then stood up and walked over to the bed and sat down.

"Man, you gotta ignore that shit the nigga was poppin'," Danny said in a rush. "He just high offa weed and actin' stupid. We cool, right, ma?"

"It's all good," Chastity started putting the duct tape, knife, and Taser back in her bag. "Let me ask you something real quick. Legend really working with that nigga Wheatie now?"

"Yeah, I don't know why, but he was the one who reached out and made it happen," Danny said. "I guess he told Wheatie the reason, but I don't know why." He gave a little chuckle. "But what the fuck I care, you feel me? Them's the big boys."

210

So it was true. Legend had turned on Hunter, and it was probably because of her. And Jackie had been kidnapped, beaten, tortured, and raped, because she had been mistaken for her. She hated herself. But she also hated Legend. Because if Legend had simply told her that he loved her, that he wanted her, she would never have fallen in love with his cousin, and none of this would have happened. But no, it was Jimmy --- Aunt Daisy's boyfriend – whom she really hated. If he hadn't raped her, she could have stayed with Aunt Daisy and never met Legend. And her hate suddenly extended to her father. If hadn't killed her mother he wouldn't have been taken to prison, and she never would have been sent to live in a foster home in the first place. And she hated her mother. If she wasn't such a slut, hadn't two-timed on a man who had been good to her, her father wouldn't have murdered her. At that moment, and for the first time in her life, Chastity was painfully and utterly aware of the hatred that had consumed her for the past three years.

Chastity picked up the gun and aimed it at Danny. *Bitch nigga.*

"Yo! What the fuck –" was Danny's last words.

'I'm getting better at this shit,' Chastity thought as she put the gun in her bag and went into the bathroom to wash her hands. 'That time I hit him just where I wanted. Right between the eyes.'

Shay

Chapter Fourteen

"**H**unter! Oh my God, baby! I've been so worried!" Chastity was so excited she pulled off to the side of the road so she wouldn't get into an accident.

"Chastity, where you at? And why aren't Hulk and Rhino picking up their cells?"

"I'm in the Bronx, Hunt. Some fucked up shit happened, babe," Chastity said in a rush. "Hulk and Rhino are dead. And Jackie's been kidnapped. And Legend's working with Wheatie. And I just killed some guy named Danny. And –"

"What the fuck!" Hulk shouted. "Chas . . . what the fuck . . . Shit! Slow down, tell me what the hell is going on. Wait. First off, are you okay?"

She took a deep breath. "Yeah, I'm fine."

"Okay, tell me exactly where you are."

Chastity looked up at a street sign. "I'm on Tremont Avenue, on the corner of 172nd Street." She heard him repeat the address to someone, and tell them to head over, and then he got back on the phone.

"Okay, now tell me everything that happened."

"Some guys burst into the house in Camden, I don't know how. But they shot Hulk and Rhino. I was hiding in the bathroom and they didn't find me, but I know that one of their names was John-Boy, and Hulk shouted out that he was driving Danny's car, and he said both of them used to work for you."

"Damn."

212

"When they left and I got downstairs, Hulk was already dead, but Rhino was still alive." Chastity took a breath. "Hunt, baby, the last thing Rhino said was that John-Boy got a call from Legend while they were still there. I'm telling, you Legend's selling you out!"

"No, he's not, but go 'head," Hunter said in an agitated voice. "What else?"

"I went over to your house, and that's when I found out someone had gotten in and broken up all your shit," Chastity paused, "And Hunt, the only person with the security code was me, you, and Legend. And whoever it was had the security code so –"

"Chas, just go 'head," Hunter said impatiently.

"Well, I got all the money out, just in case they came back, and then I saw you had some FedEx packages, I don't know why, but I picked them out. Thank God, I did, because I got in touch with your friend, Bill –"

"You spoke to Bill?" Hunter said in an incredulous voice.

"Yeah. He told me he was trying to contact you, too, but wasn't able to get you." Chastity paused. "Hunter, are you okay? Where've you been?"

"We're on our way over to where you are now. I'll explain when we get there. But what's this stuff about you killing some nigga? And what's this shit about Jackie being kidnapped?"

"Yeah, okay, so Bill told me to get some place safe, and I went over to Jackie's place. And, oh yeah, there were two FedEx packages in your spot. One had the cell phone from Bill. The other had a DVD. When I got to Jackie's I played the DVD, and it was a video saying that they had kidnapped Jackie. They thought she was me."

213

Shay

"Fuck!"

"So then I managed to find one of the kidnappers who I saw on the video and I got him to tell me where they're holding Jackie," Chastity continued, "and then . . . well, then I shot him. And I'm on my way to where they got Jackie now."

"No! Don't go nowhere. Stay your ass put," Hunter said in an urgent voice. "We should be pullin' up where you are in like twenty minutes."

"Ten minutes. We're pulling off the Cross Bronx Expressway now," Chastity heard someone say in the background.

"Hunter? Was that Legend's voice I just heard?" she asked nervously.

"Yeah, he's been handling shit behind the scenes the whole time. He was only making believe he was down with Wheatie, and shit. He let Wheatie think he was double-crossing me, then set up a phony meeting where I was supposed to get smoked, but me and my boys were waiting and we smoked them instead. But I'll explain all that later. I'm gonna fill Legend in on all you just told me, and then I gotta try and get in touch with Bill."

Chastity breathed a sigh of relief. *Okay, my knight in shining armor is on the way. Or two of them, I should say.* She wanted to slap herself for ever believing that Legend had turned on Hunter . . . and turned on her. Maybe after this, she thought, everything can go back to normal. *God, I hope they get here before those niggas start fucking with Jackie again.* She wiped the tears from her eyes as she thought about her friend.

Tap, tap, tap.

Hunter and Legend were tapping on her car door window. She unlocked the doors, and Hunter jumped in the passenger seat, and Legend climbed in the back.

"Oh, Chas, I'm so sorry about all this shit," Hunter said, pulling her into an embrace. "I feel so fucked up you had to go through all this shit 'cause of me."

"Baby, I'm just so glad you're okay," Chastity said through her tears. "I thought maybe they killed you or something."

"Shit, that nigga's too mean to die," Legend said from the backseat.

"Fuck you, muthafucka," Hunter said with a grin, while still holding Chastity.

"Right back at, nigga." Legend answered.

"Hunt, we've gotta get Jackie." Chastity pulled away from Hunter and wiped her tears. "The building they're in is only a few blocks from here. We can be there in less than five minutes. Danny said there was only two guys in there with her, but they were expecting him back in an hour, and it's been like almost that now."

Hunter patted her arm reassuringly. "I got six guys on their way to meet up with us now. They should be here in like twenty minutes. Don't worry, we're gonna handle this shit before they hurt your girl."

Chastity shook her head. "No, you don't understand. What happens if they call Danny's cell and he doesn't answer? They've already fucked her up, bad. Look!" she hit the play button the DVD player.

Hunter reached over and hit the eject button in less than two minutes. "I've seen enough. You ready to roll, cuz?"

"Fuck yeah."

Shay

Chastity looked in the rear view window at Legend. His jaw was as tight as Hunter's, and his eyes were colder than Chastity had ever seen them. It was evident he was ready to kill.

"What's the address, Chastity?" Hunter asked.

When she gave it to him he got on his cell and relayed it the men he had called earlier to meet them.

"Okay, let's roll. Chastity, you stay here in your car."

"Wait," she said frantically as he and Hunter started climbing out the vehicle. "How are you going to get in? You know they're not just going to open the door."

"We'll figure something out," Legend answered.

"But I've already got something figured out." Chastity held up a big bag marked McDonald's. "They told Danny to bring them over some food when he came." She jerked the bag before Hunter could grab it. "Look, they're a helluva more likely to open the door for me then two big ass niggas with guns."

"Chas, I don't want you invol –"

"Hunter, that's my girl in there," Chastity said, cutting him off. And the only reason they got her is because they thought they grabbed me. I'm already involved."

Legend shook his head, "I don't like this shit, Hunter."

Chastity turned to him. "Look, you got a better idea for getting in? If you niggas just try busting down the door there's no telling who's going to get shot. My way is perfect. I go in, you go in right after me."

"Better yet," Hunter said. "You get them to open the door, and we'll just go in and you just get the hell out

216

of the way. And I mean that, Chas. I can't have anything happen to you, girl."

"I promise."

"Who is it?"

"Are you John-Boy?" Chastity called out in her sexiest voice.

The peephole opened up, and an eyeball appeared in the hole. "Who the fuck wanna know?"

"Danny sent me." She smiled and held up the McDonald's bag. "He said someone in there needed some food and some good pussy for his birthday."

"Yeah?" the voice had turned from suspicious to happy. "I can smell the food, but how I know you got some good pussy?"

Chastity stood back from the door so he could get a full view of her body. Then she started unbuttoning her mid-belly blouse. "Want me to show you?"

"Girl, get your ass in here."

She could hear the sound of the door being unlocked, but she waited until the door swung open before she jumped aside.

Hunter, who was at the side of the door with his gun cocked, grabbed John-Boy by the throat and pulled him into the hallway. "Who's in there with you, nigga?" he growled in a whisper.

"No one, I swear." John-Boy's eyes were almost popping out of his head.

"I said," Hunter pressed the gun against John-Boy's forehead. "Who's in there with you, nigga!"

"Ricky! Ricky's in there, man."

217

Shay

Legend, gun in hand, walked over and patted John-Boy, but found nothing. He nodded at Hunter, than slowly moved into the apartment, and positioned himself in the kitchen doorway, which gave him a full view of the living room and of the bedroom door. Then he nodded at Hunter again.

"Tell Ricky to come out here for a minute. And if you try to warn him there's gonna be some nigga brains decorating this fucking hallway. Got that?" Hunter said, pressing the gun against John-Boy's head even harder.

"Hey, Ricky! Come out here, man. I want you to see something."

"What man? I'm trying to get some sleep." The voice came from behind a bedroom door, and Legend immediately trained his gun on it.

"No, for real. Come out here for a minute," John-Boy called out.

The bedroom opened, and the man who Chastity had seen on the video appeared. "Fuck man. Just 'cause it's your birth –"

"Put your hands over your head, muthafucka." Legend said in an even voice as he stepped into view. "Now drop to your knees."

Hunter dragged John-Boy in as Ricky complied, and Legend strode into the living room and put his gun to Ricky's throat. "Where's the girl?"

"What . . . what . . . girl?" Ricky stammered.

Legend smashed the gun against Ricky's head, pushing him backwards, and then Legend brought foot down, hard, on Ricky's groin, causing to give a high-pitched scream.

"Now you wanna tell us where the girl is?" Hunter asked John-Boy who was whimpering fear.

218

"In the bedroom," he said quickly. "In the bedroom where Ricky was."

Chastity darted into the apartment and ran into the bedroom. Jackie was hogtied, covered with blood, and feces, on a sheetless stained mattress on the floor.

"Jackie. Oh, God, Jackie," Chastity picked her up and cradled her in her arms. "I'm so sorry!"

"What?" Jackie said in a hoarse whisper. "Chas? Is that you?"

"Yeah, it's me, girl. We're gonna get you the hell outta here." Chastity gently lay Jackie back down and began untying the ropes binding her. "I got here as soon as I could. I'm so sorry about all this shit."

"Where . . . where's . . . there was some niggas in here . . . where . . ." Jackie was speaking in what seemed like a half-conscious state.

"Hunter and Legend have them in the living room, girl. They're about to fuck them niggas up."

"Hunter's here?" Jackie said as Chastity helped her sit up. "Damn, 'bout time I finally get to meet your nigga."

"Listen to you with the jokes! God, Jackie, I thought they were gonna kill you. I was afraid we'd get here too late."

"Sheeyet, even if them niggas kilt me I wasn't gonna die, bitch. I ain't drove your fuckin' Maybach yet."

Chastity grabbed Jackie in a gentle hug, and the two of them began to laugh.

"Come on, now, girl. Let me help you get cleaned up," Chastity said after a few minutes. "We gotta get outta here."

She located Jackie's clothes, though they were partially torn and dirty. Then ran and got a wet

Shay

washcloth from the bathroom and wiped her friend's battered face and body down as best she could.

"I look like shit, don't I?"

Chastity nodded. "Yeah, but you're still alive, that's what counts. Everything else can heal." They walked into the living room and found Hunter and Legend had tied their two victims in chairs and were pistol whipping them as they asked questions.

"It was Danny's idea," John-Boy was saying. "Wheatie didn't even know. Danny thought if he could get you Wheatie would move him up in the organization. I swear, Hunter, I didn't wanna go along. Danny said he would kill me if I didn't." John-Boy's head was gashed open in two spots, and one of his shoulders drooped as if it had been smashed from the socket, and he sobbed as he spoke.

"Hmph, I kinda figured Wheatie wasn't in on this shit," Legend said. "Don't make no difference now, though." He turned to Ricky, "How did you find out about the house in Camden?" When Ricky didn't respond fast enough Legend swung his gun at Ricky's mouth, smashing in four of his upper teeth, "I said, how did you find out about the house in Camden?"

"Hmph, he sure didn't find out from me!" Jackie said walking over to them.

"Hey, you must be Jackie!" Hunter said. "Now you and Chastity get the fuck outta here."

"Damn, you Hunter? Shit, Chastity wasn't lying, youse one fine muthafucking nigga."

"What? Huh?" Hunter looked at Jackie as if she were from out of space, but Legend started laughing. Chastity just smiled and shrugged her shoulders.

"Yeah, okay, thanks. Now get the fuck outta here!" Hunter said, bewilderment still in his voice.

220

"Yeah, aight, nigga we leaving. But not before I do this." Jackie ran over and grabbed Ricky's nuts through his pants, and gave them a vicious twist. "Yeah, muthafucka, you was worried about me biting it off? How about I twist it off, huh? Better yet, somebody get me a knife. I'm a cut this shit off."

Chastity walked over and grabbed Jackie. "Come on, let the men do their shit. Them niggas are going to get theirs, believe me."

"You thought I was gonna give up my girl, huh?" Jackie taunted. She turned to Hunter. "I ain't tell them about the place in Camden. I ain't tell them shit."

Hunter's eyes narrowed and he looked at Chastity. "How did she know?"

"Well...ahem..."

Legend out a chuckle. "I could have told you she'd tell Jackie. Them two are as tight as me and you."

Hunter sighed and shook his head. "You tell anyone else, Chas? Tell me the truth. I ain't gonna be mad."

"No, I swear!"

"I know how they knew. There's was some nigga named Dwayne up in this muthafucka, told them about the place in Camden and gave them the address, too," Jackie said. "And there was another nigga up in here named Danny. I guess they didn't care about me hearing their names because they planned on smokin' my ass." She smashed Ricky in the nose. "Ain't that right, you pussy-ass nigga?"

"Chas, will you PLEASE get this girl up outta here!" Hunter shouted. "Damn! She's gonna fuckin' kill them before we find out what we need to know!"

Shay

"Shit, I ain't movin' up outta here," Jackie said walking over to the sofa. "I wanna watch these muthafuckas die. Anyone got a blunt?"

Legend walked over to her. "Jackie, I really like you. But don't fuck with us on this," he said in a menacing tone. "Get the fuck outta here and get the fuck outta here, NOW!"

Chastity grabbed Hunter's arm. "Here," she pulled the Taser, and the stun guns out her bag. "This might help you out with them," she said handing them over. "Oh, and just in case you need to shoot them to make them talk, use this," she said pulling out the .38 and the matching silencer. "You don't want anyone calling the police because they heard gunshots."

"Goddamn!" Jackie said in a loud voice.

"What, you got a fuckin' arsenal in there?" Hunter said in amazement as he turned the .38 over in his hand. "Where's you get all this shit?"

"I'll explain later," Chastity grabbed Jackie by the arm. "Come on, girl."

Legend just shook his head and chuckled. "You got one dangerous woman on your hands, there, Hunt."

"Lock the door after them, cuz," Hunter said as Chastity and Jackie scurried into the hallway.

Chastity grinned as she pushed the elevator button. "You are seriously one crazy bitch, Jackie."

"One crazy lookin' one, anyway." Jackie touched her cheek and winced. "Look what those bastards done to me. They fucked me up but good."

"True –"

Jackie suddenly put her hand up over Chastity's mouth. "Wait!" she whispered. "You hear that?"

Chastity pushed Jackie's hand aside and went over to the banister and listened. She could hear voices come from the first-floor.

"I recognize one of the voices," Jackie whispered. "It's that Dwayne nigga."

"It sounds like there's at least three motherfuckers with him, maybe more." Chastity said back.

The elevator had just reached their floor, and Chastity quickly opened the door, took off one of her shoes, and jammed it so the elevator couldn't close or move. Then she rushed back over to the apartment and tapped on the door. She waited until she saw the peep hole open, then motioned frantically for Legend to let them in.

"I thought we told you, to –"

"Sh!" Chastity rushed past him, pushed Hunter aside and pulled the duct tape out of her bag and ripped off two pieces, placing them over Ricky and John-Boy's mouth. Then she turned to Hunter. "There's at least four guys on their way up here," she said quickly. "Jackie recognized one of their voices as Dwayne's."

"Fuck!" Hunter said as he walked over to the door. "Jackie, is there a fire escape in this mug?"

"I don't know. Let me look."

Chastity could hear the elevator buzzing, which meant the men downstairs now knew it wasn't on its way to get them. They'd be heading up the stairs in any moment. In fact, Chastity could already hear them running up the stairs, laughing and cursing.

"There's one outside the bedroom window," Jackie said rushing back in the living room, "but there's an air conditioner in the window, and it's too heavy for me to move."

223

Shay

As Hunter strode inside to remove the air conditioner, Legend took the .38 and shot Ricky and John-Boy in the throat. He was heading into the bedroom when the key turned in the lock and the front door swung open.

Chastity watched from the open bedroom door as Legend took aim and fired. The first man coming through the door fell back with a bullet to the chest, knocking him into two of the men standing behind him. "Get the girls outta here," Legend shouted to Hunter as he took aim at another man. He got two more shots off, but then one caught him in the shoulder. Instead of rushing into the bedroom, though, he retreated further into the living room, drawing the fire away from Hunter and the women. Jackie was already on the fire escape, and Chastity was climbing out the window when she turned toward the doorway and saw a bullet hit Legend's head. She screamed as he fell backwards on the floor.

Hunter jumped into the living room firing his .45 automatic, yelling, "You muthafuckas," at the top of his lungs.

Looking down to make sure Jackie was safe, Chastity climbed back into the apartment, ducking down below the line of fire. She scrambled on her knees into the living room, pulling the .45 she'd taken from Hunter's safe out of her bag. But by the time she got to the room the shooting was over, and she saw Hunter crouching over Legend's body, crying. Tears welled up in her own eyes, as she called out to him. He turned, and she was walking toward him when, to her astonishment, he raised his gun in her direction.

"Hunter, no!" she screamed, trying to dart out the way as he fired. But instead of hitting her, the bullet

slammed into a man she didn't know until then was standing behind her. A man who managed to get off one last volley of shots from his automatic rifle before he fell to his knees; a volley that lay Hunter's stomach open, and his intestines spilling out. The man, though he seemed to be dying, took aim again, but before he could squeeze the trigger, Chastity shot him in the head.

"Oh Jesus, Hunter!" Chastity screamed as she ran over to him. "Hunter, baby, you're going to be okay. I promise. I'ma get you to the hospital."

"They . . . fuckin' . . . killed . . . Legend. They . . . killed . . .. my cuz. But . . . you're . . . okay . . . right, baby?" Hunter said through closed eyes.

"Sh, don't try to talk. I'm fine. And you're going to be fine, too.

"No you . . . get . . . outta here." He opened his eyes and tried to smile. "I seen . . . you shoot that . . . muthafucka. Legend was . . . right . . . I got me . . . one . . . dangerous . . . bitch."

Now that all of the shooting had stopped a crowd of tenants were beginning to form outside the door. Crying, Chastity searched for her bag and pulled out her cell phone to call 911, but before she could dial, six or seven uniformed police rushed in, guns drawn.

"Put your hands over your head, and get up slowly," one of the officers said, his gun trained on her.

"We need an ambulance. He's still alive," Chastity said, pointing at Hunter.

"I said, put your hands over your head!" The officer shouted.

"Hold on, I got this." A white man wearing a black suit and sunglasses, walked in front of the officer. "Agent John Robbins, CIA," he said flashing a badge. "We've been investigating this gang for months now."

He reached into his jacket and pulled out a walkie-talkie cell phone. "Jimenez, get up here, quick." Robbins put the walkie-talkie back into his pocket. "Has the scene been secure yet?"

"Listen, this is our bust," another uniformed man with stripes on his shoulder said.

"Sergeant," Robbins looked down at the man's name tag, "Sergeant Meadows. Agent John Robbins, CIA." He flashed his badge again, then gave the police sergeant his business card.

"Agent Anthony Jimenez, CIA," another man with a dark suit and sun glasses said, walking up and standing next to Robbins. He flashed his badge then looked at Chastity. "Has she been read her Miranda rights, yet?"

"Look, we've got to get an ambulance. He's dying!" Chastity said frantically. "Please, I'll cooperate. Just get him to a hospital."

"We got here same time as you, so we haven't read anybody anything yet," Sergeant Meadows said. "But this is the city of New York, and this is our crime scene and we don't want –"

Robbins held up his hand. "Understood. There's not going to be any fight about jurisdiction. Just let me ask her a few questions, before you take her downtown." He looked at Jimenez and said, "Read her her rights and cuff her."

Jimenez grabbed Chastity and threw her against the wall, pulling her arms behind her back and snapping on handcuffs as he spoke: "Jennifer Williams, you have the right to remain silent."

Chastity turned her head and looked at the agent in surprise. "I'm not –"

226

He pressed her back further into the wall, almost cutting off her circulation as he continued. "If you give up this right anything you say may be used against you in the court of law . . . "

'What the hell is going on? And who the fuck is Jennifer Williams?' Chastity wondered as the men finished reading her the Miranda Act.

"Sergeant Meadows, all clear, sir," one of the unformed officers said.

"Good," Robbins said brusquely. "If it's all right with you, Sergeant, we'd like to take Miss Williams into one of the rooms for a preliminary questioning before you take her downtown. You'll be taking her to One Police Plaza, I presume?" He looked around. "You want me to get a couple of my men over here to help secure the scene? We can't afford to have any of the evidence compromised."

"The New York City police know how to secure a scene, Agent," Sergeant Meadows snapped. "Question her in there, if you want," he said pointing to the bedroom, "but she's riding with us when you're through."

Robbins nodded. "Understood, Sergeant." He motioned to Jimenez, who grabbed her by the arm and walked her into the bedroom.

To her surprise, once she got inside and the door was closed, Robbins put his hand over her mouth and said, "Be quiet. We're friends." He unlocked the handcuffs while Jimenez put a chair underneath the doorknob. Then he walked her over to the window, and helped her climb out, with him and Jimenez following.

"No," he said as she started down the escape, "We're going up."

Chapter Fifteen

"Girl, I'm sorry. I was waitin' for you around the corner, but when I heard the police sirens I haul-assed outta there," Jackie was saying. "And I ain't had a dime on me. I had to jump the fuckin' subway turnstile."

"I woulda done the same," Chastity said sullenly as she soaked in a bathtub full of silky bubbles in her apartment. "That shit was crazy."

"So if they weren't really CIA, who the fuck were they?"

"Hell if I know. All I know is once they got me back to my car, they handed me a cell phone and told me to drive off. Then Bill called –"

"Who the fuck is Bill?"

"See, I can't quite figure that shit out, either. I don't even think that's his real name," Chastity said, throwing her hands up in exasperation. "All I know is he's a friend of Hunter and Legend's. But he obviously works for some kind of federal agency, and he's got a lot of pull. Hunter called him before we got to the building to let him know what was going on, and he must have sent those guys for back up for them." Chastity paused. "Only they got there too late."

"So what did Bill say when he called on the cell?" Jackie asked.

"He told me to tell him everything that happened. And then he said, okay, he'd take it from

there. He's supposed to call me back as soon as he finds out where they're taking Hunter."

"Damn," Jackie sighed and pulled a drag from the joint she's been smoking. "I can't believe Legend is dead. I mean, this shit is unreal."

Chastity sniffed as she tried to blink her tears, wondering why her tear ducts even still worked with all the crying she'd been doing all day and night. Still, it was over. Or almost over. *Hopefully Hunter will pull through and we can start our lives over again.*

Both girls jumped when they heard the doorbell ring.

"Should we answer it?" Jackie whispered.

"I don't know." Chastity got out of the tub and grabbed a robe hanging on the bathroom door. They looked at each other as it rang twice more. Then the cell phone, lying on the bathroom sink began to ring.

"Hello?" Chastity whispered.

"It's Bill. Open the door."

Chastity rushed into the living room and let him in. "Is he okay? Is Hunter, all right?"

Bill walked into the living room and looked at Chastity, the sadness of his expression telling it all. "I'm sorry."

"Oh, God!" Chastity collapsed on the floor, and Jackie rushed to her side.

"Oh, Chas, I'm so sorry, girl. Come on, now," she said, cradling Chastity in her arms. "We're gonna get through this, Chas. We still got each other."

"And," Bill walked over and gently pulled Chastity up from the floor. "And, you still got Legend."

Chastity drew a sharp breath. "What do you mean?"

Shay

"Come on over here and sit down," Bill said, guiding her to the couch. He looked at Jackie. "Maybe you should get her a drink?"

Jackie nodded. "There's some Moet in the frig. I'll get a glass."

"Well, I was thinking of something stronger," Bill said gently. "Maybe some brandy? Whiskey?"

"I think she got some apple brandy up in here," Jackie said, nodding her head towards a small bar in the corner. "I'll get that, but talk loud so I can hear what y'all sayin'." She frowned when she saw the look on his face. "Shit, she's gonna tell me later, anyway. Save her the fuckin' trouble!"

"Well, when my men got there and assessed the situation, they immediately called for an ambulance, one of our private ambulances –"

"Who the fuck is y'all that you got private ambulances?" Jackie demanded as she searched for the brandy and a glass behind the bar.

"Well, luckily our ambulance guys got there first," Bill said, ignoring her. "From what I was told they thought Legend was dead at first, too, but they found a weak pulse, and took him off with Hunter. He's got a severe head wound, but they don't think there's any brain damage, and chances are he'll pull through. If we're lucky, he'll be out of the hospital in just a few days."

"Oh thank God," Chastity said, taking a sip of the apple brandy. "Can I see him?"

"Not yet. He's unconscious anyway," Bill said. "But I'll send a car to take you to him tomorrow. But it's important that you don't disclose his location to anyone. Right now, there's nothing to connect, you, Hunter, or

230

Legend to the scene. We're going to try to keep it like that."

"But, ay, yo, don't the hospital have to notify the police of any gunshot victims?" Jackie asked.

Bill smiled. "Not our hospital."

Jackie threw her hands up, "Word. This shit is crazy. You got your private ambulance to take people to a private hospital, that doesn't report to the police. Who the fuck are you guys? For real. You can tell me. I ain't gonna say shit to nobody."

Bill smiled. "The less you know the better. You're Jackie, right? How are you doing?"

"I'm a little fucked up, but don't worry I don't need no private ambulance. A couple of drinks, a couple of joints, a couple of days, and I'll be fine." She narrowed her eyes at him. "You ain't with the DEA or anything, right? I was only kidding about the joints."

"You don't have to worry about me." Bill turned his attention back to Chastity. "What about you? Do you need me to send a doctor over with something to help you sleep?"

Chastity shook her head. "No, but you can do something else for me."

"What's that?"

"Well, since you seem to be so good at cleaning up messes, well," she cleared her throat. "Well, I kinda have a dead body that needs to be, uh, picked up or cleaned up, or whatever." She quickly told him about Danny's body still tied up in a chair in the midtown motel room. "You think you can handle that for me?"

"Shit, you sliced him, diced him, and shot him, too?" Jackie grinned and reached over and gave Chastity a dab. "My girl."

Shay

"No problem. Anything else I need to know about?" Bill said calmly.

"Well, I broke into someone's apartment and, uh, borrowed their gun. But I don't think we'll have to worry about it," Chastity said slowly. "He likely won't know it's missing for a few days, and even then he won't know it was me who, uh, borrowed it."

"Damn!" Jackie said.

Bill raised his eyebrow. "Anything else?"

Chastity took a deep breath. "What about Hunter's body? We're going to have to arrange for a funeral."

"Yes, but don't worry, I'll help with the arrangements. And we're going to have a private doctor —"

"There he go with that private shit, again." Jackie shook her head.

"We're going to arrange for a private doctor to sign off on a phony death certificate saying he died from a heart attack. No autopsy will be needed, and we'll have to have the funeral – closed casket, of course – at one of our funeral parlors."

"A private funeral parlor, no doubt."

Bill ignored Jackie. "But like I said, we'll make all the arrangements. And if you want to have a public memorial service later, let me know and I'll have someone help with those arrangements, too. Of course, I won't be able to attend."

Chastity nodded. "Of course." She let out a sigh. "Bill, thank you so much for everything. You really are a good friend."

Bill stood up. "Hunter would have done the same thing for me. He was a good man." He walked over to the door, but stopped before turning the knob.

"Oh, and one more thing. Your lawyer, Gephardt, will be getting the rest of the pictures and documents he needs on Monday. That should be more than enough to win your father an appeal."

"Damn," Jackie said after he left. "Is there anything that nigga can't do?"

"God, Jackie, I can't believe that Hunter's dead," Chastity shook her head dismally.

"Yeah," Jackie gulped down the rest of the brandy in Chastity's glass, then poured herself another. "And I can't believe that Legend is alive."

Chapter Sixteen

"You going to be okay, Chas?" Legend said as they left the graveside memorial service.

Chastity nodded. "It was good meeting your parents. I'm just sorry it had to be under these circumstances."

"Yeah, how about that? I'm going to go ahead and take them back to the airport." They walked in silence to Chastity's car, a new Maybach which was delivered just two days after Hunter's death. Jackie was behind the wheel, and she gave them a somber smile and wave as they approached.

"I told you I'm having a mausoleum built for him, right?" Legend said. "The biggest one in this cemetery. Shit, the biggest one in New York."

Chastity smiled. "Hunter would have like that. And listen, I still have that money –"

"What money?"

"The money from Hunter's air conditioning safe."

"How much was it?"

Chastity took a deep breath. "It took almost a whole day for Jackie and me to count it, but it came up to a little over six million dollars."

To Chastity's surprise, Legend didn't seem fazed by the amount. He simply nodded and said, "You

keep it. And I'm joint on his overseas accounts, so I'm going to break you off some of that, too."

Chastity shook her head vigorously. "No, uh uh, I was his girlfriend, not his wife. Let that money stay with his family."

"Shit, ma, you know if he lived you woulda been his wifey."

"But he didn't, and I'm not," Chastity said adamantly. "I'll keep the six million, and thanks for that, but the rest of it is for the Fosters. Hunter would have liked that."

"Chas, I'm going to call you on my way back from the airport, okay? Do you think it'll be alright if I stop by?" Legend looked down on the ground. "I know it's soon, and I want to take things slow, but if there's one thing I've learned over these past few weeks, it's that we can't waste time waiting for the 'right moment.' If we do it'll come and go, and just pass us by." He grabbed her hand and put it to his lips. "I don't want to get passed by again."

Chastity looked up at him, at those deep penetrating eyes that had almost hypnotized her on the very first night at the club. There was a sadness evident that had never been there before. A sadness that matched her own. But there was also a longing there, that reached out to her, and this time, she was going to be damned if she didn't reach back.

"Legend, I'll be waiting for you," she said tenderly.

"And I promise, this time I won't keep you waiting long."

PREY FOR LOVE – Leyton Wint

All he needs in this life of sin, is his gun and his girlfriend.

Not only does Alex "Lex" Walker kill people for a living, but he's good at what he does. Skills and discipline has Lex at the top of his game and the gig in Miami seems to be just another step towards retiring rich. That is, right up until he crosses paths with Chaine, a mysterious sensually daring beauty who's got all the right moves and the curves to match.

Love isn't on his agenda, but Lex soon finds himself caught up. Distracted by an intense love affair, Lex is unable to see that the girl of his dreams just might be his worst nightmare. As the lines between business and personal get blurred he finds himself on a wild ride fueled by sex, exotic locations, and gunplay.

In the world of murder-for-hire hitting your mark means the difference between survival and starvation, and falling in love is a liability that could cost everything. The game that once showed him love threatens to take Lex under. It's a fight for his freedom, fortune, and his very life; as the predator becomes the prey.

www.myspace.com/preyforlove

Harlem Godfather: The Rap on My Husband, Ellsworth "Bumpy" Johnson

Forget Nicky Barnes and Frank Lucas, when it came to Harlem the undisputed king of the underworld was, Ellsworth "Bumpy" Johnson.

He was called an old-fashioned gentleman. He was called a pimp. A philanthropist and a thief. A scholar and a thug. A man who told children to stay in school, and a man whom some say introduced heroin into Harlem.

Bumpy used his fists and his guns to get what he wanted, but he also used his money to help those in need. To this day – forty years after his death – people still sing his praises.

And no one more than his 94-year-old widow, Mayme Hatcher Johnson, author of *Harlem Godfather: The Rap on My Husband, Ellsworth "Bumpy" Johnson.*

Read the real story of the larger than life Bumpy Johnson, who was portrayed in the blockbuster movies *Cotton Club, Hoodlum,* and *American Gangster.*

Find out Bumpy's *real* relationship with Frank Lucas. And learn the story of a real man -- who never snitched – and loved as hard as he fought.

www.harlemgodfather.com